Seeking Clarity

Beverley Courtney

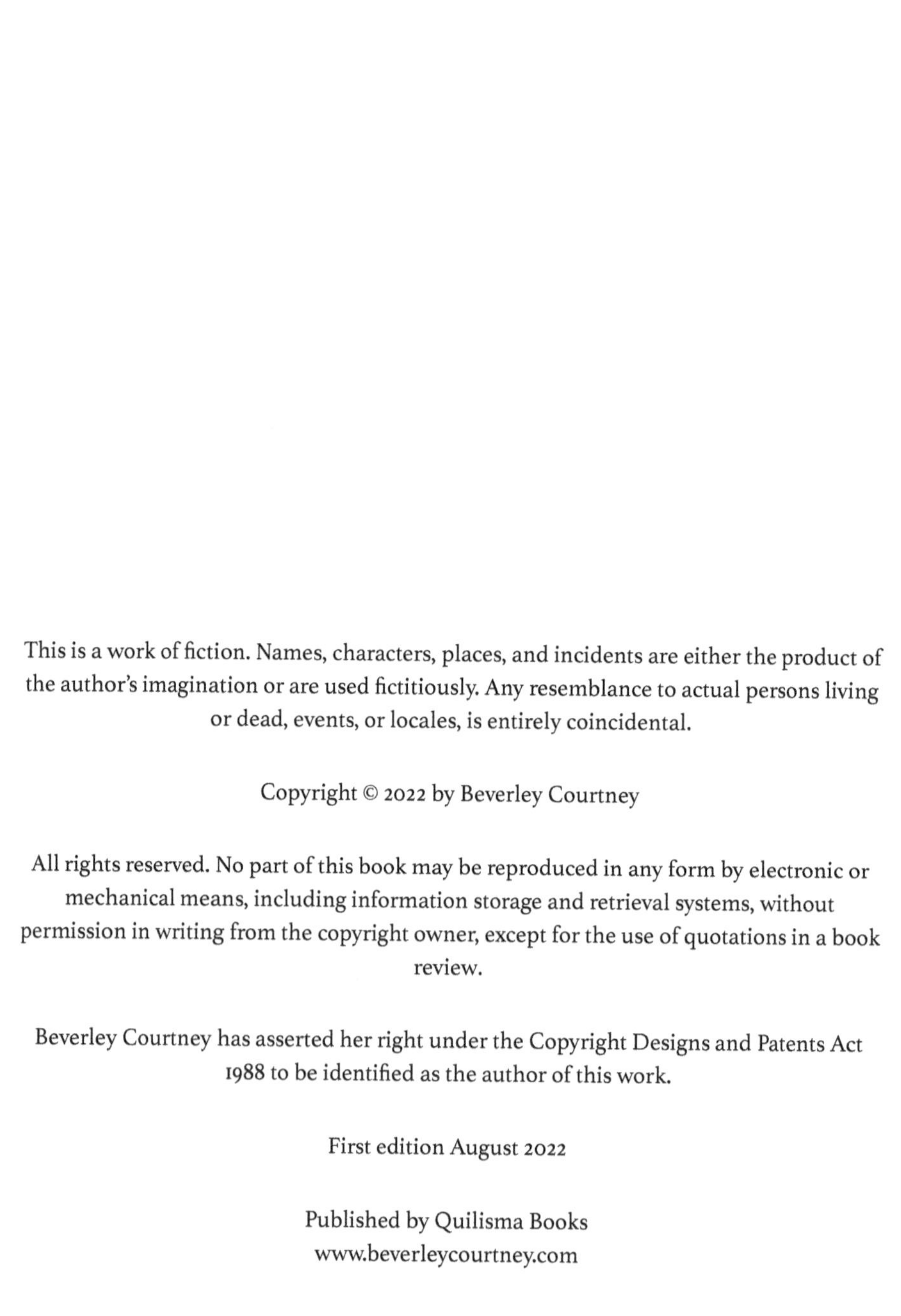

First edition August 2022

Published by Quilisma Books
www.beverleycourtney.com

Also by the Author

Keeping Tabs
A Women's Fiction Novel of Doubt, Dogs, and Determination
(Dilemmas and Discovery series, Book 1)

and the complete **Brilliant Family Dog** library
on Dog Training and Behaviour

1

Clare stretched out her long legs and admired her shoes. Fabulous, impractical shoes she'd bought with her own money. She tilted her head to look at her Editor and said, "You're absolutely right, Joanne, I do love writing pieces that get into people's souls. I'm not interested in their surroundings except how that affects them." Clare was in her Editor's office to discover her latest assignment. As a freelance writer for Zenith's glossiest of glossy lifestyle magazines, she didn't often visit the Holy of Holies. It transpired that her task was to interview the young celeb Echo and write about her new pad – a thoroughly renovated listed Manor House in the countryside. Thing is, the scandal surrounding the rising star had been so public that even Clare had heard about it. Echo had recently fallen foul of the tabloids with the usual story of sex, drugs, and rock and roll.

"So," Clare waved her hands expressively, "while I'm sure Echo's home is amazing and beautiful and has won loads of design awards - I'm more interested in why Echo feels the need for this backdrop. What image does she think this home projects about her? And why has she got herself into such a public mess? That's what I want to get at!"

"That's why I chose you to do this piece," replied Joanne, nibbling thoughtfully on the arm of her huge red glasses, which as so often were not on her nose, but being twiddled in her hand. Her Estuary English contrasted sharply with Clare's soft Irish lilt.

Clare glanced through the wall of office windows at the view of the city below as a couple of seagulls flitted past, probably screaming - though she couldn't hear them through the thick glass. The building was not that far from the river. She sat up straighter and leaned on Joanne's desk, a glass and chrome contraption that fitted the image of the glamorous lifestyle magazine she edited, but was woefully lacking in practical qualities. Like desk drawers for instance. Everything got piled up on the shelf behind Joanne's chair, in precarious mounds that threatened to cascade down on her head.

"Thank you!" Clare said, genuinely excited and flattered. "It's just the kind of piece I want to get my teeth into. I'd like to look at Echo - in fact, any famous iconic person - from a more human viewpoint. It's not even clear that she's done what they say she's done. It's easy enough to believe that a pop star has drug-fuelled sex romps. But maybe it's all news hype? I want to see what makes her tick. Find out what she really feels, when the cameras aren't on her."

"I hope I'm not going to get warnings from the legal guys?" smiled Joanne.

"No, don't worry. I don't want to disembowel her, or show her up. I want to find out the real Echo. She's obviously amazingly gifted - that latest song of hers is beautiful - and she seems an interesting prospect for a piece. It should warm more people to her. I'd really like her to *like* what I write."

"You certainly have a gift for getting info out of people, Clare," Joanne replied, putting her glasses back on her nose and studying her. "That piece you did about that drama friend of yours ... she seemed a bit of a nobody, but you managed to make her very interesting, and reveal that there was much more to her than met the eye."

When she had first arrived back in England, with the zeal of the freshly-converted, Clare had relished helping her friend Tabitha with her marital situation - a situation in fact so much worse than Clare's own had ever been. She smiled softly as she thought of her old friend Tabs emerging from her chrysalis as a beautiful butterfly, even now still discovering her gifts. "Well, we go back a long way," she said, "No way would I shaft her!"

"You may want to revisit that subject in a few more months. A follow-up. It would be good if we could see how she's grown into her new situation - now she's a success, and how that success is affecting her."

"Deal!" said Clare eagerly. "I'll hold you to that. I know she's flying, and I'd love to do a follow-up. Thanks!" She smiled inwardly, and allowed her smile to show outwardly too, as she took a sip of her coffee. She was proud of the part she'd played in securing her friend's freedom.

The aroma of good coffee was something Clare could never tire of. And she always bought a couple of cups of specialist coffee on her way in to Zenith to bring to her meetings with Joanne. Joanne had appalling taste in coffee, and Clare not only didn't want to share what she offered but she wanted to try and convert her to something better. The truth was that either Joanne glugged it down without thinking or she left it to go cold. From seeing her at events, Clare knew Joanne really preferred something pale and bubbly in a glass. But at least Clare benefitted from a decent drink.

As Clare made a note of her initial 'Echo' thoughts in her notebook – perhaps she'd use the angle of the gifted singer swept away by schemers, a girl manipulated by powers that she couldn't comprehend - she also added a note to revisit the Tabitha story. Joanne folded her big red glasses, put them down on the desk, then picked them up again and continued twiddling them. "I'd like to have some more pieces about *less* famous people. People more relatable to our readers. What they could become if they put their mind to it, sort of thing."

"I'd love that!" Clare waved her pen with enthusiasm. "I talked a lot with Tabitha, that drama friend, when she was struggling, and really it was all in her head! Everything that wasn't working was coming from thoughts she was having, not fact. We re-jigged some of those thoughts and suddenly she became a capable go-getter." She put her notebook and pen down on the desk. "That's something I'd really like to get into: I was thinking of a book ..." she added, a little nervously. "Of course when I've got my own column that will be easier," she laughed, looking anxiously at Joanne and hoping she hadn't pushed too far.

"O-k-a-a-ay. Put that on the back burner for now while you dream up some ideas to bring me."

Clare hid the jolt this gave her. She'd been hoping for a little encouragement from her Editor, whose skills and nous she respected. And a word from Joanne would go a long way with potential publishers! But as a jobbing writer she knew she had to prove herself repeatedly first. She wouldn't mention the book again - just get the thing started. Joanne sifted through one of the mounds of papers in front of her and pulled out a couple of sheets. "Now, the next project I want to go over with you ..."

"Not the wife of another disgraced politician?" laughed Clare. "Or is it someone who seems to have more children than he's owned up to ...?"

They fell to discussing the new subjects Joanne wanted her to pursue. Since Clare had arrived at the magazine eighteen months before, she'd managed to make quite an impact with a few "lucky breaks" as she had called them. But Joanne had told her, "I can recognise talent when I see it," and had made it clear to Clare that it was her tenacity, her approachable manner, and her undoubted writing gifts - her easy style which managed to convey deep thoughts - that was winning the day.

"You've got it, Clare," she'd told her. "You can do this stuff. You don't have to try so hard."

"I don't want to stand still any more," Clare had replied with fervour. "I've wasted so many years - I'm determined to forge ahead now, make a name for myself."

She'd explained her marital set-up - or current lack of it - to Joanne when she was still quite new. And Joanne, who saw herself as a bit of a crusader for downtrodden professional women, was happy to give her her head.

"This is your moment," Joanne smiled at her protégée. "Don't miss it."

The magazine got quite a postbag about Clare's human interest stories, and their online platform made it easy for them to track their popularity. That was information Clare would love to use, so she could show publishers she had an eager readership that would snatch up a book if they had the chance. As the whole printing industry lurched into the 21st Century with all its technological advances, it may have lost a lot of the old traditions of printing ink and paper, some of which had entered the language - like the individual metal capital letter forms being stored in the Upper Case of the shelving, and the small letters in the Lower Case - but there were definite advantages to working online, with all the analytics they could use to drill down through the reading figures and stats, and understand and serve their audience as well as they could. The advertisers loved it, of course, as they could refine their targeting. But it worked for the content, their messaging, too.

Joanne liked to stay one step ahead of her audience's demands, and she was happy to have landed Clare, who seemed to appeal to so many of them.

Twirling her red glasses again, she added, "And I want to talk to you about syndication too. There's a lot more you can do there. Have a word with Chris in Circulation. He knows all about it. There are right and wrong ways to go about it, like with everything else. You know what a big international readership we have - especially with all our different titles. I feel we could appeal to a lot of ex-pats with your approach. With your background, you're not as insular as many of our staff writers."

Clare's background had been one of her selling points when she first arrived at the mighty Zenith Publishing House. She'd started her job-hunt by applying there because it was the best fit for her, and where she'd envisioned her writing career going, as well as being one of the biggest in the business - owning most of the Lifestyle shelf. 'Might as well start at the top and work down,' she'd said to herself. And despite her confidence in aiming high with her first attempt, no-one was more surprised than she was when they accepted her first three articles, then invited her in for discussions. She didn't have the depressing experience of 'tramping the streets' - albeit by email these days - doing the rounds of all the possible publications, and the dispiriting rejections. It's true she'd gone through quite a few of those when she was still at home - her old home, before she made the decision to leave to start her new career - to leave her comfortable 18th Century mansion, its equestrian business, her duties as Chatelaine, and her family, in order to devote herself wholeheartedly to her passion. She knew in her heart that the only way she could succeed at anything was to devote herself totally and exclusively to it. And when it came to single-mindedness, there was no-one to beat Clare!

Zenith liked that she was a mother, and that her children were grown and out of the way. They liked that she had been the hostess of a large country house in Ireland, entertaining, and living the country life that so many of their readers aspired to. They liked her easy professionalism, her appearance which was business-like yet entirely natural - a kind of marrying of business attire and cream- and heather-coloured cashmere jumpers and casual trousers. She had a classless elegance that conveyed good taste but didn't alienate. They liked that she knew everyone who was anyone in Ireland - many of whom also lived in England, indeed all over the world as is the way with the Irish - with connections, through the two sides of her family, to the literary world as well as the farming and horse-racing people. A kind of Irish Aga life. The plush look and message of a top-of-the-range range, but with the scent of smoking peat - or turf as the Irish call it - that evocative homely smell you only find in Celtic and Scandinavian countries. So she had been firmly pigeonholed when she first arrived. Now Clare was beginning to break out a little, slowly but surely flexing her writing muscles and her imagination.

With her straight, shoulder-length, light brown hair - her mother always called it "fair hair", while Clare preferred "mouse" - her willowy figure, and forthright manner, she appeared confident as she strode into interviews, and dealt ably with technical problems. She was glad to have kept her girlish figure - "I'm very fortunate with my genes!" she'd say - and she was well aware she looked much younger than her years. She had a ready smile, and while she knew well that men responded particularly well to her warm manner, she didn't put women's backs up, as so many journalists could. There were advantages to being brought up in a friendly Irish backwater, where the ability to get on with all types and levels and ages of people was a skill she had had to learn young.

For these reasons, Joanne had been glad to snap her up and claim her for Zenith. And she'd been an immediate hit.

"There's one other thing," Joanne added as Clare rose to leave. "I want to nominate you for the industry Social Impact Award. I think a few of your pieces fit the brief well."

Clare stopped in her tracks, and gaped at Joanne. "Really?" was all she managed to say. "Thank you Joanne! I appreciate your confidence in me.

That's exciting! Ooh, thank you!" She left the Editor's office grinning broadly and treading on air - her decision to focus single-mindedly on her writing career was beginning to pay dividends.

She strode purposefully through the long office full of desks and busy people. Well, most were busy, though some still had time to chatter or gaze out of the office's huge windows with the city spread out below.

What a different view from the one she had grown up with. Here there was hardly a blade of grass in sight. Where she grew up there was hardly a building in sight.

The Long Room, as it was known, had its own particular scent - a smell of busyness, coffee, and possibly of carpets overdue for a deep clean.

"Hey Clare!" said Nat, one of the sports journalists, as she neared his desk. "Been to beard the dragon in her den?"

"Hi Nat!" Clare laughed, turning away from the windows. She knew that Nat admired Joanne, for all her fearsome reputation. "You bet! And she's putty in my hands. Seriously, I'm walking on air right now ... my plan is beginning to work out! How's it going with you?" Clare had always liked Nat since he'd fetched her a coffee when she was waiting to meet Joanne for her first job interview. She was nervous and he'd helped put her at her ease. He liked to talk about his children, and ever since, she'd always been happy to encourage him in this.

She perched herself on the corner of Nat's desk while she smiled at him, ready to listen to today's story. He wasn't the sort of person that she thought she'd like but, as it happened, she really did. He reminded her of the humble folk in County Kerry where she'd grown up. Above all else they valued their family: that was the most important thing to them, keeping the family together. And nobody was better at keeping extended families together than the Irish, even across borders and across oceans. And they took a simple pleasure in what their family did. Nat was very like that.

Nat watched her settle to listen. "Exams." He replied tersely. "Both girls are in exam years. It's really making life a strain at home ..."

"Poor you! I remember that stage, though mine were a bit further apart in age so they didn't both hit exams in the same year. Thank goodness." She raised and dropped her shoulders at the memory. "But it won't go on for ever. It'll pass. Mine are off my hands now, thank heavens! Both settled at university. Heads down studying. Best place for them."

"You're referring to this 'life after children' people talk about?" said Nat with a crooked smile. "Does it really exist? Or will I die before we get there?"

"Yes," she laughed, and theatrically wiped her hands, "I've done my bit, rearing the next generation. Time to focus on myself after twenty-odd years of looking after everyone else!"

"But don't you miss them?" asked Nat in wonder. "I do love having them at home - the whole family vibe, you know."

"I don't have time to miss them." Clare smiled at Nat. "There is more to life, really!"

She hopped off the desk, swung her bag over her shoulder and said, "And I'm off to enjoy some more of it right now. I've got a lot of years to catch up on - it's me-time now! See you, Nat!" She strode, still smiling, down the length of the office, and waited for the lift.

As the lift arrived, one of the several people who got out was her occasional boyfriend Nick. Nick worked in Events and was untrammelled by family, having shed his a good few years back. He made phone gestures to her as the crowd of hurrying people swept him away, talking noisily, and Clare took their place in the lift. "Sure!" she called with a broad smile, as the doors began to close, "Give me a ring ..." It was a good, easy, relationship she had with Nick - no ties, for either of them. No commitment, just fun.

She hugged her arms around her in a moment of pleasure. Her life was her own again, and she was ready to enjoy every moment. It was just a question of keeping everyone in the places she had allocated them - so they didn't interfere with her grand plan - and convincing Joanne by her outstanding pieces that she was worth more than these popular celebrity page-fillers. One day she'd get that column! Only then would she be seen as an artist in her own right. Only then would she have reached her dream.

2

Clare arrived home with a couple of bags of food shopping. She loved the variety of shops here in the city and enjoyed making interesting meals for herself in the evening. With no-one else's tastes and requirements to take into account, she was able to have what Tabitha's young friend Melanie referred to as 'walnuts and toast' - whatever she felt like eating, instead of the meat and two veg every day without fail that Melanie's father required. Being able to eat walnuts and toast was a rare treat for her.

Clare was not eating walnuts and toast tonight though. She'd bought the ingredients for a Thai curry and was fingering the lemongrass and enjoying the scent it gave off as she unpacked it all in the kitchen, when the phone rang.

"Hi Nick," she said as he greeted her, "that was quick! You weren't kidding ..."

"Had to catch you! I've got a great opportunity for us - didn't want you to miss out on it," replied Nick a little breathlessly. From the background noises he must have been walking along a busy street. "It's an event I have to cover next week. It's the opening of that new super-duper hotel in Surrey, very expensive. It's all on expenses of course, so I wondered if you'd like to come? I'll be working, but we'd be able to spend some time together - it's been a while, Clare ... and you may pick up some useful contacts there too, of course."

Clare got the lowdown on the event and the exact dates from him and pondered. It was several days away - no rush. She guessed that the urgency was in Nick's mind. If she refused, he wanted to have time to find someone else to enjoy the visit with. Fair enough, she thought. Their come-and-go relationship was very much 'no strings attached'. So she had no problem accepting the invitation. Who knew how many he'd already asked!

"That will be fun," she said. "There could well be some interesting possibilities for me amongst the guests there. I'm looking forward to it already!"

Scribbling the dates in her diary, she returned to the kitchen. Truly she had it all! She was still getting used to the strange feeling that success in this new field gave her. Sometimes she felt regrets ... but not for long. Her star was rising, her work was being acclaimed - nominated for an Award! - she had friends, boyfriends, and zero commitments. She was on her way to getting that column she so coveted, and entering the most influential part of her life: what a change from all those years before!

"Be a good girl now and lay the table, Clare," her mother would say. "Put those books away and take your turn with the mending basket!" "Those potatoes aren't going to peel themselves, girls." Clare smiled, leaning on her kitchen worktop, knife in one hand and shallot in the other, as she remembered the layers of service being built into her psyche early on. Everything was done to make the home run smoothly so her father, the eminent poet, could work undisturbed by such minutiae.

And once she was married and had children to rear, this became her life too. Jonathan came first, and the children came second. Clare came nowhere. She spent a lot of time and effort being the perfect hostess for Jonathan's vast crumbling pile of an ancestral home, forever managing decoration projects and organising the outdoor staff (one old gardener and his boy) to defend the ornamental gardens from being reclaimed by the wilderness beyond the Pale.

The stables and the gallops were managed by the stable staff, and Clare was mercifully spared any involvement with them. The whole place was pristine. She would smile as she thought of the contrast between this countryside and the countryside in Kerry she was reared in – battered gnarled oak posts lurching at strange angles; gates held together with baler twine; gaps in hedges filled with rusting discarded farm machinery; shed doors furnished with old car-door handles. Here the fenceposts were soldier-straight, the gates perfectly aligned with never a squeak, the hedges trimmed neatly and efficiently, the lawns could win competitions.

So her domain was everything but the demesne. She operated largely indoors, the chatelaine, arranging the endless dinner parties, accommodating foreign business guests, preserving the image of the well-to-do country house. But while these duties and the family kept her fully occupied, this was never what she felt she was born to do. So her frustration had grown and grown. It wasn't till the children were teenagers that she felt able to carve out time for herself from her wifely duties and start on an Open University degree, there in the Morning Room of her home. Once the children were both at boarding school, she had much more time for herself, and happily immersed herself in her studies. Emerging from the four years of head-down studying, she had a named degree for creative writing, which showed her particular area of expertise, and a huge sense of achievement. She was proud to add the letters after her name.

Jonathan regarded all this work with vague amusement.

"How's the *magnum opus* going?" he would tease.

"You'll be sorry when you read it and find it's all about the perfidy of racehorse trainers and race-fixing," she would laugh back with him.

It was harmless banter and she still laid on lavish dinners for his clients and colleagues - other racehorse owners and trainers - so he was happy enough. It would take Clare a good couple of weeks to adjust when the children came home on holidays. She found she had to limit herself to a set number of hours writing and reading then put her things away and switch to family duties. Fortunately, like most teenagers, they slept late every morning when they could. Rollo and Marigold were both approaching independence fast, and seemed to be managing the teenage years without undue upheaval. But Clare knew the clock was ticking, and made efforts to enjoy their company during these times - all the while the idea was taking form in her head of her impending escape and transformation. She'd achieve her dream at last, of becoming a celebrated and respected writer, like her father!

In her very own kitchen now, she sliced the shallot, remembering how that idea had appeared, taken shape, grown - until it became inevitable. She was made for more than this! She was her father's daughter. She wanted to create, not stay stifled in domesticity. And this is what had driven her to where she was now. Living in a city, writing pithy articles and in-depth appraisals, enjoying mixing with other creatives, relishing the fast city life.

Nick was one of several boyfriends. She spread her favours evenly and without commitment. She wanted to have a good time, in good company, and had no plans to get tangled up in anything that would nail her down or limit her in any way. As Jonathan had been her first and only partner ever since she was a teenager, this was new and exhilarating. She smiled with pleasure as she chose some music to accompany her cooking.

It was a while later, having enjoyed her delicious non-walnut meal, that her phone beeped and Rollo's face appeared on the screen.

"Hi Mum!"

She beamed at her older child: it was always a pleasure to see him. " Hi to you!"

"We-e-e-ll, I thought you'd be pleased to know that I'm on track for the Best in Year prize."

"Wow!" Clare enthused with a glow of pride. "Tell me more!"

"It's to do with consistency. Best marks overall, kind of thing. My Tutor told me yesterday that he could see no reason why I wouldn't get it if I carry on as I am."

"Congratulations in advance! I'm proud of you, whatever you do or don't achieve - I think you're a marvel! So tell me, what are you focussing on this year?" Clare had long since learnt not to ask more specific questions about Rollo's work. He was studying Electrical Engineering and Applied Maths, and the first few times she'd asked him what it meant he started to tell her, only to have her say, "Stop! I don't understand a word. You're simply a genius - let's leave it at that!" She did try to wrap her head round what he was saying, but resigned herself to the fact that the artistic side of her brain far outweighed the scientific side.

They chatted for a while and Clare felt warmth rising up within her. How was this brainy and good-looking boy hers? She told him about her Editor's remarks and the Social Impact Award. "So it looks as though we may both be celebrating in a few months' time," she added, happily.

"Have you heard anything from Marigold," he asked as they were about to ring off.

"No, not recently. She's all set to start her second year - I gather she's sharing a house this year, not in Hall. She's very self-sufficient - she'll be in touch in her own good time."

"Oh, ok," Rollo replied. "Just wondered ..." he tailed off. "Well, bye anyway," he added cheerily, and the picture went black.

What did he mean by that? thought Clare. Marigold was certainly the more complex of her two children, but she'd understood everything was going smoothly for her. She was studying Irish and its literature at Trinity College Dublin - a chip off the grandfatherly block, as Clare's father had held the Chair of Poetry there, back in the day, and had been a renowned Irish scholar himself.

She thought back to his rooms, on the ground floor of the old university building, with the lawns outside the window criss-crossed with paths full of busy students scurrying from one class to another. He'd loved entertaining there, and had organised a lavish tea for her on one of her last visits to him. As if she were still a child and he was still her father.

She shrugged and set about checking over her diary for tomorrow. She had her first meeting with Echo the next day, and she spent a while working out the journey times and deciding what she would wear before taking herself to her blissfully empty bed and settling into its comfort. Top quality cotton bedlinen was one of the first things she'd spent money on when she'd moved to her own home. Money so well spent, she smiled, as she stretched and snuggled into a deep, contented, sleep, thinking of the promise of the exciting day to come.

3

As she drew up at the electric gates of Echo's mansion, Clare woke a gang of *paparazzi* from their doze. They swarmed round the car, their cameras in front of their faces, popping pictures.

"It's ok, guys," she said, as she wound down the window to address the little keypad on a pole in front of the gatepost. "I'm nobody famous - just one of you." She answered the crackly voice that came from the speaker without having to give her name, and as the gates slowly whirred open, she waved cheerily at the disappointed photographers, who plodded back to their camping chairs and vacuum flasks with a resigned air. That another journalist had got an interview while they were parked on the verge outside the gates was a story they would not be passing onto their editors!

The drive was worthy of the house it reached. It was long and winding, along an avenue of youngish birches. As she emerged from this cover to the front of the house to park in the large gravelled area in front, she puzzled over the age of the building. It seemed to be what you'd expect a listed manor house to be, except that everything was new, gleaming, smart. It was large but with pleasant proportions, a soft reddish brick framing the large sash windows. Like the grounds that she'd driven through, it was unassuming, pretty, and expensive. While you're not allowed to alter the outside of a listed building, you can make hay indoors - so Clare looked forward to getting inside and having a look.

"Are you the journalist from Zenith?" asked the thin woman holding onto the front door, waiting for Clare to ascend the stone steps.

"Clare O'Sullivan, yes," Clare smiled her most charming smile, and waited a moment till the woman said, "I'm Echo's mother. You'd best come in."

"Are the hounds baying at the gate giving you a lot of trouble?" Clare asked with genuine sympathy as she offered her hand.

"They're all driving us mad," responded Echo's mother. "They have no feelings ..." She showed her into a large and comfortable living room before sliding silently away.

Clare stood in the middle of the large and beautiful room, absorbing the atmosphere. She recognised the artists of some of the large contemporary paintings Echo had on the walls, knowing some of them from articles she'd been involved in writing. When Echo made an entrance - she had that star presence that could never allow her to just seep into a room unnoticed - the two women hit it off straight away. Echo looked very little as Clare had expected from her performing persona photos. Her usually spiky blonde hair was smooth and wavy, and instead of a flamboyant and revealing garment, she wore a simple white polo-neck jumper and light blue trousers.

"You've met my mother, Linda?" said Echo, as they sat enjoying the coffee and tiny homemade biscuits Echo's mother had set before them, before she started to evaporate again.

"I have! Thank you, Linda." Clare gave her most expansive smile to the woman as she retreated, realising Echo's mother was maybe not suspicious as she'd thought, but merely shy, and protective of her daughter. "Now," turning to Echo and clearly showing her recorder before placing it on the coffee table between them - she knew she was dealing with a person experienced with the press and the media - "tell me more about your lovely home."

"I love being surrounded by beauty," responded Echo quickly. "That's why the room is laid out to draw your gaze through the french windows to the fantastic view." Clare followed her glance to see distant blue hills framed by the natural woodland of the garden - now red and ochre in its Autumn colours. She could imagine how lovely it would look in the Spring, with the sharp bright greens of new leaves. "I need nature around me," Echo gazed longingly at the view. "Hate the city. I like everything I look at to be pleasing - though of course, beauty is in the eye of the beholder, as Mummy will often remind me!"

Clare indicated the largest of the paintings and asked, "Do you paint, yourself?" as she jotted Echo's words about beauty down in the notebook she liked to use as a backup to her recorder, to mark significant details. "You know Constable said, 'I never saw an ugly thing in my life'? You seem to be on the same wavelength."

"I do actually - paint, I mean. I didn't know about Constable. I love that!" Echo looked down at her hands in her lap. "Though I don't do anything like these," she swept her arm to indicate the large paintings. "I like to draw, really - using lots of colour. I like combining the precision of drawing with the emotion of colour ... but perhaps you'd better not write all that down," she said, lifting her chin to peer towards Clare's notebook.

"I'd like to mention how artistic you are. Would it be ok to just say you like drawing?"

"Yes. It's a private part of me. I don't want anyone to see what I draw."

"Got it," said Clare, making a note in her book, and dramatically crossing out the words above it. "Though I do want to be able to show some of what you're like when you're not on stage, in the public eye. There's a lot to you, and it would be good for people to remember you're a human being, not public property."

Echo put her cup down slowly. "I know this is a PR exercise, and it's the price of fame. But I do want to keep as much as possible private ..."

"You come over as a very genuine person, who happens to have been blessed with enormous gifts. That doesn't mean you belong to your audience! But I can convey my impressions of you without giving too much away. I really will respect your privacy."

Echo smiled back at her with a look of gratitude.

Clare noticed that the star's lightly-made up face showed a clear skin, and along with her soft, shiny hair and her trim figure, none of it suggested somebody who is in the grip of some addiction - on the slippery downward slope of drugs or drink, the way the tabloids had claimed Echo was. She warmed more to her.

It wasn't long before Echo was opening up to Clare, appearing to forget that this was a magazine interview. Clare's pencil worked busily, taking down gems as they poured from her subject.

She explained where the gutter-press stories had come from. "It was a hare started by a disgruntled backing singer. It's true there are people in the business who do these things - but I don't! I want to keep my feet on the ground and enjoy my career. It was horrid, and I never realised how badly it would affect me. I had to cancel several engagements - I just wasn't up to it."

"I'd like to present the side of Echo that the public, in its feeding frenzy, seems to be missing," Clare reassured her quietly. "That behind the public persona is a genuine person who needs time and sensitivity - a creative woman who is sensitive, who loves beauty, who draws. I get that in your business you have to portray a certain type of person - rebellious, outrageous - but the way you're put forward to your public is very different from ... you."

Echo's mother was with them again, hovering like a bird protecting her nestling. Not a forthright character, she spoke in a brittle voice, clearly reciting words she had been planning.

"My daughter's been through a lot. I do hope you're going to be true to your word, and not hang her out to dry again, like the others have done."

"Mum!" exclaimed Echo, blushing.

"It's ok, I know just what you mean," responded Clare quickly, holding up her hand as she recognised the hurt in the mother's eyes, the same hurt she saw in her own mother's eyes at the break-up of her family. "My interest is in showing the woman who loves beauty, who is fallible like the rest of us, but has so much more to offer. There have been times in my life when I've felt vulnerable, and just having someone listen meant so much to me then. Understanding and acceptance can come later. But being heard is important."

Mother and daughter looked at each other, and the mother relaxed visibly.

The crunch of tyres on the gravelled drive signalled the arrival of the photographer with all her gear.

"There's Harriet - our photographer," said Clare, looking over her shoulder to see the familiar car. "I'd really like her to capture some images of you looking thoughtful and reflective, perhaps drawing one of your pieces, or walking in the garden. Not brash, smiley, images. More confidential, one-to-one type of pictures. Do you get what I mean?"

"I'd like people to see the softer side of me," agreed Echo, who had clearly grown to trust Clare during their conversation. "I think you're right. So often they just see the extrovert performer image. They just seem to want the 'sex, drugs, and rock and roll', and it's time they saw that there's more to me than that."

Clare nodded, standing to greet Harriet as the photographer was shown into the room by Echo's mother, on door duty again. Harriet - always appearing busy - lowered her various black bags of cameras, tripods, and lights, to the floor and offered her hand to Echo with a friendly smile.

Clare explained the brief to Harriet, and while she was busy getting her gear out of all its black bags and assembled, Clare drifted over to one of the large bookcases in the room. She picked out a book and flipped it over, surprised that it was some kind of self-development book. She put it back and on the shelf and ran her finger along the spines of some of its neighbours.

"It was a friend who introduced me to these," said Echo, coming up to stand beside Clare. "He took me to a seminar given by one of those famous ra-ra type people. The guy's ability to manipulate a large audience was captivating. I thought I could use some of his techniques for my own performances, you know? So I decided to do a bit of research." She fingered several books, tipping them out of the shelves just enough to show their covers. Her favourites, perhaps, thought Clare as she made a mental note of their titles.

"You've certainly done that thoroughly - there are at least two shelves here devoted to the subject!"

"I found a good few authors I liked. I've actually got to know some of them. There are advantages to being famous," she grinned.

Harriet took over then, discussing her ideas with Echo. "I'll start with some indoor photos on that sofa, showing the paintings behind if that's ok with you? I think a light blue garment would look good against the white sofa. Have you got something like that? Then we can explore the garden. It looks beautiful! Are you the designer? Or perhaps you like the earth under your fingernails?" They moved away, heads together, planning the session. Harriet had a way which was both professional and friendly. "They have to trust me," she'd explained to Clare on their first assignment together.

All the clothes changes and setups took time, and Clare settled down in one of the large sofas with the fresh coffee Linda had brought her, and a handful of the books from the bookcase. There was certainly a big disconnect between the public perception of this singing star as the usual kind of show-off forever kicking over the traces, and what Clare was learning today.

She took the opportunity of Linda bringing her coffee to comment on Echo's name. "Echo? Such an unusual name!"

"We honeymooned on a Greek island - so romantic." Linda smiled as she gazed into the distance, revisiting that Greek island, its sunbleached houses, its brilliant turquoise sea ... "And it wasn't long before I found I was pregnant. So a Greek nymph seemed a good inspiration." As she topped up Clare's cup she added, "I'm afraid it did cause a bit of teasing at school - but now it's such a fitting name that people think she made it up!"

Clare fished her pinging phone from her pocket. "Ah, and there's *my* daughter!" she smiled to Linda, dropping the phone back in her pocket to deal with the text later.

And so the visit was a resounding success for both Clare and Echo. Clare had a notebook and recorder full of information and interest, and from what she'd shown her on the tiny screen of one of her cameras, Harriet had captured a number of excellent images of Echo, some forthright, some whimsical and reflective. Clare was already looking forward eagerly to making this into a large, penetrating, article. She felt pleased and fulfilled as she left the house a while later, waved off by Echo and her mother, both of whom gave her a warm goodbye. It was a rare gift she had, she reflected - though the Irish charm she'd been bathed in for so many years certainly helped!

She set her GPS for her next destination and drove away down the long drive, waving to the annoyed paparazzi as she sped away through the open gates. She had got the prize they all were hoping to snatch - that rare glimpse behind Echo's façade.

When she'd awoken in the morning, Clare realised that her journey would take her not a million miles from her mother's home. As she'd waited for the coffee to get itself ready she had debated with herself whether she'd visit her.

Like many mothers and daughters, they had a relationship which ranged from extreme devotion to violent frustration. Both strong characters, differences of opinion could be marked, and Peggy would often end a discussion by pulling the "mother" card. Clare alternated between 'Ma', 'Mummy', and 'Peggy', determined by her degree of dependence at the time. Once she was married and distanced from the family, her father had always preferred her to use his Christian name, probably to disassociate himself from the relationship with this erring daughter.

It was a while since Clare and her mother had last met, though there had been phone calls from time to time. Clare had felt the pangs of duty and decided she'd look in on the way back this afternoon. She had texted her mother with her plan, and in moments a message had pinged back: "Darling! Can't wait. I'll get some buttermilk scones on the go!"

After all her deliberation, the deed had been done. Clare was glad, and while she didn't exactly look forward to the meeting - there were always mixed emotions - she looked forward to having had it. Even while she forged ahead with her beginning-to-glitter career (as she told herself) when she would truly be her own person, she felt keenly the duty of keeping in touch with her mother.

So she felt a warm glow of achievement as she headed to her mother's - she felt she was on her way to her goal. It became clearer to her by the day. She was working so hard now, because she knew she'd be truly happy when she was an acclaimed journalist and author, could spend her time writing, and devote herself to the creative side of her personality, without having to worry about anyone else! It was that complete single-minded focus and purpose that drew her on. It was all ahead of her and she would not stop striving till she got there.

And she felt sure her mother would have something to say about that …

4

Another driveway, another beautiful country house - though this one was very much more modest than Echo's, more a cottage than a manor house - more like the Kerry farmhouse Clare had been reared in than the mansion she'd married into. Peggy still enjoyed growing things to eat as well as to enjoy looking at, and had a traditional cottage garden where cabbages mixed with lavender, marigolds peeped out between pea-sticks, and the contented clucking of foraging hens could be heard from the back of the house. Clare enjoyed visiting this comfy home, and she appreciated how much her mother loved it. But she had no wish to return to any kind of rural life herself. She was happy with her flat and her city view - nothing to have to bother with, minimal upkeep. She hated the feel of earth under her fingernails, as Harriet had suggested to Echo, and saw gardening as outdoor housework, and was glad there had always been gardeners on the staff at Brownestown.

Another mother greeting her at the door. But this time not with averted, suspicious, eyes, but with a warm hug and a beaming smile. Clare found herself the child again. The young girl whose Mammy was the answer to all ills. She wondered for a moment if her own children felt this about her? Rollo seemed to, and kept in touch regularly, but Marigold was very distant at the moment. She sighed, abandoned those thoughts, and focussed on herself being the visiting child. It was a pleasant and comforting state to drift into - but she knew she'd be drifting right out of it again as soon as she left. And perhaps beforehand, if things got fraught!

"Clare. Darling. So wonderful to see you again. You look terrific!" said her mother, beaming from ear to ear as she welcomed her into the house. "How did your interview go?"

"It was great, Mummy. Echo's really a very interesting person behind all the hype and glamour. I'll enjoy writing it up."

"Make yourself at home - I'll just get the tea ready," cast Peggy over her shoulder as she headed to the kitchen.

Clare went over to the fireplace and spent some moments looking at the painting hanging above it - a traditional painting in contrast to the bold contemporary work over Echo's fireplace. It was a view of the spectacular landscape of the Ring of Kerry, with lowering clouds and sparkling green fields below, painted by a friend of theirs, back in the day.

She had had a traditional Irish family upbringing right there, in County Kerry, on the wild West coast of Ireland. Peggy was English but had met Clare's poet father Michael when she was studying at Trinity College, Dublin. Clare knew that her mother had quickly been assimilated into the Irish lifestyle, sucked in like so many by the charm and feyness. And, her own career abandoned, spent her time rearing her five children - of which Clare was the eldest - and baking bread, growing vegetables, milking goats, making cheese ... It was an idyllic childhood in a ravishingly beautiful but harsh landscape. The slightly hippie nature of their home meant that the children were encouraged to call their parents by their names. Clare had never been able to do this till she was older, but she liked it now. It made her and her mother more like equals, friends, rather than one always being in thrall to the other. Her father she had never called Michael till long after she'd left home. And curiously, she reflected that her own children never called her by her name. The painting brought that life flooding back into Clare's mind - the sights, the sounds, the scents - remembering long days mucking out goat pens (warm hay smells), swimming in the stream (cold and shivering, sandy feet), packing milk and eggs to sell at the gate (carefully weighing, measuring, and spilling), weeding the lazy beds - nursing the potato rows (aching back and those muddy fingernails).

She heard the clatter of mugs and plates from the kitchen, and smiled as she thought of the pleasure her mother always took in feeding folk.

As a child, Clare had learnt that women were secondary beings. That men ruled the world and women should count themselves lucky to serve them. Her younger brothers had a very different life from that of her sisters and herself. They were part of the ascendancy and got waited on too - though they did have to weigh in with "manly" jobs about the house, like fetching the coal, chopping logs, driving the donkey cart to town, and so on.

Clare had always lived in awe of her father Michael, the celebrated poet. She loved that he was devoted to his art while the family scurried around making his path smooth, giving him everything he needed, from home-grown and lovingly-cooked meals to ironed shirts and a clean writing room - and mostly peace and quiet and distance from the harsh realities of daily life.

"Quiet now!" was a common cry from Peggy to the children when they got noisy, "Your father's working." Clare had learnt early on that her father's work was sacred, that his creativity was the most important thing in their lives, that their place was to honour his gifts and allow it to flourish.

The oven door banged as the sweet smell of Peggy's scones drifted into the living room.

Her mother had made virtually all their food from scratch as they grew up. Their own eggs, milk, cheese, meat, vegetables, and what fruit grew on their exposed hillside. She'd juggled the finances and made most of the family decisions, like where the children should go to school, while Michael had the last word on the more abstract matters like who they should vote for, what they should believe in, and whether the children should go to school at all. He felt that children, in the main, should be seen and not heard. Children, in this case, meant the girls. "Is it a boy or a child?" people would ask when hearing of a new baby. Clare was a child, and learned it very young.

She peered more closely at the painting. There was a group of children playing in the hedgerow of one of the further fields. Boys, and children.

This ethos of serving had spread into Clare's adult life. It wasn't meant to. She'd had grand plans as a young girl of being a literary sensation, like her father. She pictured that she would attend conferences, hobnob with other literary sensations, win awards. She could imagine people would pause as she passed by in the street, saying hurriedly to each other, "Isn't that Clare O'Sullivan, the famous author?" When her younger sisters were playing house, and her brothers were outside being farmers and building things - their sticks guns to fight the Black-and-Tans, albeit many years too late! - Clare would see her own efforts at drawing and writing as being far more significant. Her father did encourage her, albeit with some amusement. But the expectation was that she should marry and produce and nurture the next generation. She was after all, only a "child".

Another bang of the oven door and a clatter, and the scent of the scones became even stronger. While she'd had kitchen staff in Brownestown, Clare had carried on the tradition of baking for the children. But it was a long time since she'd brandished a wooden spoon. No loss there, she smiled to herself.

The painting recalled her. After a brief foray to the local National School, where all the rural children mixed together in the most equal of educations, she remembered with amusement when Michael had had an argument with the Master one night in Byrne's ("Wool, Music, Beer" was writ large on the end wall of the pub-cum-shop) and pulled all his children out of the school, making a substantial impact on the roll numbers. Thereafter they lived a fairly wild and magical existence on their own land which ran down to the sea. When the land had been carved up by the Land Commission a century before, tenant farmers had been given an equal chance of the same quality land by giving them a thin strip from the top of the mountain down to the shoreline. So swimming and sailing were skills they picked up early on, along with riding the donkey, minding the hens and goats, cutting and drying turf from the mountainside for fuel, building makeshift shelters, knowing where to find mushrooms, berries and other such wild foraging. It was left to Peggy to teach the younger children to read and write.

Clare had known she was getting a poorer education than she wanted, and would sometimes get brave enough to argue with her father.

"But I'm going to go to University, Da," Clare would explain carefully, wondering if now were the right moment to broach the subject. "I'm going to be a writer, like you!"

Pleading to be able to go back to school fell on her father's deaf ears, and it wasn't until her mother had finally had enough and left for England with the children that Clare got her wish and was able to go to school again. That was where she'd met Tabitha, in whose life she had taken such an important role just last year. She was pleased to have helped her. Poor Tabitha - lost and alone. Clare, with her strong sense of purpose, would never need help like that for herself!

She heard her mother calling from the kitchen, "Tea or coffee?" and turned away from the painting and back to the present. She went to join her, chose coffee as usual, and leant back against the old-fashioned wooden worktops as they chatted.

"I was thinking back, Mum, to when we lived that charmed life in the depths of the countryside. A self-sufficient lifestyle, they'd call it now. It's amazing what we did without any of the mod cons."

"We had a few more there than when I was a girl! Course, way back then we had very little money," said Peggy as she prepared the tray. "Everything was make do and mend. You know, you didn't just throw things away like you do these days. My mother, for instance," here she put her hands on the worktop and gazed into space, "she mended everything. Nothing got thrown away until it would be mended ten times. She even turned collars on shirts back to front, so that you could get the new fabric on the underside to act as the top side. Can you believe it? And as for darning socks - who would darn socks these days? I can remember my mother saying, 'I don't care where I go when I die, as long as they don't put me in the needlework department'. She'd really had enough."

Clare reflected that she would certainly have had enough, after only one sock. Domesticity was really not her thing. She was made for something greater.

"Mum, I can remember you always with the sewing basket beside you, or the knitting basket or the mending basket. Sometimes you even just embroidered for fun."

"Yes, I always used to like working with my hands. And I couldn't sit still and listen to the radio and not be doing something. So, yeah - you children, every single jumper that you had was one that I made. And your father. He loved my Aran jumpers - went with his Irish genius poet image."

"So what do you think, would you change the old days for the days we have now?"

"I certainly would not."

"Well, I wouldn't like to survive for a moment without my washing machine!" laughed Clare.

"Yes, the convenience we have these days is absolutely amazing. But we had good things then as well - and I think of the time we spent together. There wasn't the pressure of time that there seems to be now. It was more relaxed. We just enjoyed *being*, and the simplicity of life." She looked at the laden tray and added another teaspoon. "It does certainly add plus points for simplicity. Everything doesn't have to be so complicated."

Clare knew well that Peggy always had an agenda. She seldom said anything that didn't carry a deeper message. Was she having a little dig now at Clare's abandonment of home and family in pursuit of glamour and glitz?

She looked up at Clare. "I loved being at home with you children. It was the best time of my life - even though your father was a bit bats and wandering here and there, and coming out with his strange ideas of how we should all live. It was a good time."

Here was a statement with no secret message. And Clare received it as it was meant.

"I think you gave us the best childhood we could possibly have had."

"Ah, bless you Clare!" Peggy looked at her, genuinely overcome.

"And that's what I thought of when I was bringing up Rollo and Marigold. I wanted to give them that same feeling of security of being in the countryside and feeling safe. That lovely feeling in the winter, with the excitement of Christmas approaching - when it's dark outside, and warm and cosy and safe inside. When I think of it it makes *me* warm and cosy inside!"

"Well, of course you had it very different, with all your horses and motorcars. I mean we had ... what did we have back in Kerry? We had that old banger that Dad used to use to go to the university, and we had the donkey which we would use for our messages."

'Messages', laughed Clare to herself, thinking of the Irish way of talking about running errands. Presumably because no errand was complete without an extended chat with the person being visited.

"So how's Rollo?" asked Peggy, placing jam and butter on the tray next to the soft-scented scones.

"He's doing well, Mum. In line for some prize this year. I was talking to him only yesterday. I don't really know what he does: sometimes he starts telling me but I'm afraid I just don't understand any of it," Clare smiled, leaning forward to pick up the laden tray and carry it through to the living room.

"So you talked to him yesterday - did he visit you?"

"Only on a screen!" laughed Clare. "We use the computer to talk."

"Amazing," reflected Peggy. "I come from a time when you could talk to someone on the phone for three minutes before a voice would interrupt and tell you you had to put more money in to carry on speaking. How the world changes ..."

"But some things never change," said Clare as she sat down on the sofa and helped herself to one of the fresh-baked scones. "I remember eating these by the dozen as a child."

"Yes, you all loved my buttermilk scones. I'd bake them every day in that battered old range," smiled Peggy happily. "And what about Marigold? How's she doing?" Clare wondered if she caught a touch of tightness in her mother's voice. Had Rollo been talking to her as well?

"Ah. Marigold." Clare put down her plate and leaned back in the armchair. "My complicated one. Well, as far as I know she's fine! You know she's starting her second year at Trinity now. Goodness knows, Irish Language and Literature is an esoteric subject alright, but it seems to suit her. She wants to take after her grandfather, and be a romantic poet, I think."

"God help her," muttered Peggy, under her breath.

"She does a lot of visiting ancient archaeological sites too - Tara, Newgrange, Dun Aengus ..."

"Doon where?"

"Dun Aengus - you know that prehistoric fort on Inis Mor that's half fallen into the sea?" Seeing her mother's baffled look she added, "The Aran Islands, Mum! She goes there so she can follow ley lines and commune with faeries and God knows what. She's Irish to her core!"

"But you haven't talked to her recently?" Peggy persisted.

"No." Clare carried on with her scone. "Actually she texted earlier - I'll look at it later."

"Maybe it's important? Aren't you curious? Shouldn't you at least read it now?"

Clare felt the slight irritation she tended to feel with her mother. She was like a dog with a bone. Once she'd unearthed a tasty morsel she couldn't put it down. She wouldn't be brushed off the subject easily.

"I'll check it later. She'll be in touch again if it's important, you can be sure. She's pretty self-sufficient."

Peggy sat back, unconvinced. "What about a boyfriend? Has she one of those?"

"I don't know. I don't think she has a boyfriend, though maybe she has some Druid or poet in tow. Our Marigold is made of stern stuff," laughed Clare lightly. "She's doing just fine. Oh, I didn't get a chance to tell you! I'm up for an award!"

She became more animated as she chattered on about herself, the magazine, her work, her successes, the fun she was having. Peggy listened dutifully, but with slight agitation - still apparently stuck on her previous question.

Her mother appreciated hearing her stories, and added some of her own about the rest of her far-flung family. "Like Marigold, Young Michael is also being truly Irish, but in his case by getting as far away as possible from the place. Did I tell you he's moved from Maryland to Oregon now?"

"Dad's been dead for years now, Mum. When is Michael going to stop being 'Young Michael'?"

Her mother turned and gazed towards the painting over the fire. "I can live in my dreams a little bit longer," she said, quietly.

"You know," she said brightly, sitting forward and pouring them both more coffee, sloshing cream liberally into the cups, "in the heel of the hunt, family is all we've got."

Clare looked at her thoughtfully. She knew this was one of her mother's teaching moments, and wondered what had brought it on. Was she not allowed to enjoy her own career?

"I'm glad you're doing so well in your work," added Peggy, sitting back again with her coffee, "truly I am. And I'm proud of you. I get a thrill when I open your magazine and see your name in print."

"You read my magazine?" Clare laughed, surprised.

"Course I do. But I don't want to lose the girl I love. This I know, and know full well: you'll never get the life you want if you chase success. My success was invested only in one thing - my family. I lost a lot by doing what your father dictated. Don't repeat my mistake!"

Clare picked up her coffee cup. "You think I've made a hames of my life?"

"No, no, not at all. You've done so well - especially when I let you down so badly." She paused while she thought of another time, a time in the past. "But I want to see you fulfilling yourself - in every way possible. And I know to my cost, that neglecting your family is going to come back to bite you, especially as you get older." With this she turned and gazed out of the window at her chickens pecking about the flower beds, happily demolishing flowers along with the insects.

"I'm anxious about Marigold, that's all, I suppose." Peggy got up and moved about the room. "I see so much of you in her," she added, turning to look straight into Clare's eyes.

Clare wondered what Peggy and Rollo were seeing and she was missing. Was she blinded by her single-mindedness? Did she have to interrupt everything - right now when she was in the flow - to minister to Marigold? What was this guilt her mother was heaping on her? She resorted to annoyance to counteract any shame.

So the visit was heavier than Clare had anticipated when she had started out that morning. Despite any differences she had with her mother, and keeping in touch with her out of duty and curiosity, she had expected more of the prodigal daughter welcome and less of the third degree. And she spent a lot of the long journey home reflecting on all she'd learnt that day. Her piece about Echo was going to be a humdinger! She was going to win that award. And Marigold had better not stir up trouble and interfere with that! Whatever Peggy was sensing about the child, Clare couldn't be dealing with it right now.

5

So much was whirling about Clare's head on that drive home that she felt the need for a bit of space. So she pulled off the main road onto a quiet turning, and drove till she found herself on a knoll with a sweeping view over fields and woods and what promised to be a pretty sunset.

Something was nagging at the back of her mind. And once she'd stopped the car and was gazing at the scenery, it pushed its way forward.

Ah yes! She remembered now.

They were all in the dormitory. Clare and her classmates, fifteen years old and on the cusp of womanhood. Montserrat, it was called. All the dormitories in their English boarding school were named after Marian shrines - Lisieux, Guadaloupe, Lourdes. To keep God on your mind all the time, even when sleeping - especially when sleeping - she reflected now. That was what it was like being at school in a convent.

They were meant to be asleep, but they had been whispering in the dark, free to talk to each other at last without being timetabled to within an inch of their young lives, released from the long regimented hours of lessons, prayers, exercise, and study. They kept their conversation low to avoid being heard by the duty nun patrolling the corridors, telling her beads. Penny was nearest the door and was the official lookout, listening for soft footsteps and the swish of the habit, keeping an eye on the crack of light below the door for shadows.

Susie launched the subject of tonight's chitchat: "Ok everyone, what are you going to be doing in ten years' time?"

Veronica jumped in straight away. "I'm going to be a nun."

"No-o-o!" they all cried in a whisper, "You can't possibly mean that!" "Don't do it, Veronica!" There was a spirited discussion about how becoming a nun was abdicating from life and how no good could possibly come of it. It was no better than a death sentence.

"So who's got something sensible they're going to be?" asked Susie, bringing the group back to order and to her chosen topic.

"Well," said Penny, "I'd like to have a big family with loads of children. Just like mine now, only bigger."

"That sounds ok I suppose," said Gilly. "Better than Veronica's plan," they giggled again, as Veronica sighed, pulled her rosary noisily from under her pillow, and turned away from them.

"But pretty boring," added Yvonne, in her louder, raspy, deep-voiced, whisper.

"I want a rich husband as well to go with it all," added Penny quickly. "Then I can swan around doing what I want and not have to be washing socks all day."

"That figures," said Susie, thinking of the line of white ankle socks over the washbasin. The girls liked to wash their socks daily, not wait a week till Laundry Day, when they had to run the gauntlet of Sister Maria, guardian of the Linen Room, to plead for more than two pairs of socks for the week.

"How about you, Yvonne? What are you going to be in ten years' time?

"Oh, I'm going to be a sex bomb," came Yvonne's husky voice, "and I'm going to be so much in demand ... I'm going to have fleets of boyfriends following me about. All of them rich like Penny's guy. I only want rich ones."

They suppressed their giggles under the bedclothes, so as not to be heard in the corridor.

Clare was sitting up in her bed, plaiting her hair. "What about you, Susie? What are you going to do?"

"I want to be an explorer! Africa, South America, China - all these amazing places! I want to go exploring. I can think about having a family later on. I have to get this exploring done first while I'm footloose and fancy-free," Susie turned to the quietest of them and said, "What about you, Tabitha?"

"Well, you know me! I just want to do drama. I want to act, work in the theatre. That's all I want to do."

"No family, then? No husband?" asked Penny.

"Oh yeah, that as well. Definitely! I'd love a warm family home like I had when I was little. Children, a dog and a cat ..." Tabitha smiled to herself in the dark, and her listeners could hear her smile in her voice. "Just like that. Only I want to be doing drama as well. I'm probably not good enough to be an actor, but as long as I'm involved in the theatre, I'll be happy."

"You get a bit weird when you act, anyway," Yvonne cut in, "It's like you become someone else."

"That's the whole idea, you daft ha'porth!" laughed Gilly. "I'm going to be a scientist, as you all know already. I'll go to Cambridge and do amazing research to curb disease. Those microbes are so fascinating ..."

"Yeah yeah," said Penny, "we know!"

Gilly shifted about in her bed, and decided not to respond to the gentle mockery. "So it only remains for you to spill the beans, Clare. What are *you* going to be doing in ten years' time?"

"Oh, I know exactly what I'll be doing!" responded Clare with an all-knowing tone. "I will be a writer - in my garret. Probably not earning much. But as long as I've got enough to survive on I'm ok. I'll be mixing with lots of arty types - Bohemians - artists, writers, musicians. I don't mind as long as they're creative. I'll spend all day working or fixing the world over coffee with my friends. Heated debates. Stuff that will feed our genius, give us subjects to work on." She warmed to her theme, as she started to "write" her future out loud.

"And what about family?" asked Penny. "Are you going to have a family?"

"Nope," said Clare. "They'll drag me down. They'll stop me creating. I'll be gloriously alone, carving my path."

"I suppose you're thinking about your father, the poet - the *famous poet*," said Susie. "But how does he manage?"

"Well he's got Mum. Mum does all the work looking after us kids, while he sits in his shed and writes. And goes to University, and lectures, and does important stuff. That's what I want to do."

Penny and Tabitha protested together: "You're prepared to give up having a family?" said Penny, "in order to create?" added Tabitha.

"Absolutely," said Clare. "It's the most important thing to me. That's what I'm going to do."

"Better find yourself a wife, then," said Yvonne, and they all snuggled under the bedclothes giggling, ready to dream of their exciting futures.

So when had she lost this vision? Clare knew only too well. Despite being dedicated to learning, always with her nose in a book at school, she also loved parties and fun, and the temptation of boys. And it was partying and fun - and one boy in particular - that had got the better of her and landed her in trouble.

She carried on gazing at the view from her car, as a long skein of hundreds of geese flew overhead in a ragged V, heading for their sleeping place. She could hear their distant honking, their life straightforward, their actions predestined, guided by inbuilt mechanisms they never questioned.

Once she had got back into education again, after a few years of home-schooling or, in reality, no-schooling - Clare had set her sights on a glittering university career. She saw herself starring in debates, gaining a First, all the while being the life and soul of her coterie. She worked hard through her secondary school years, so keen to impress her absent father, who was still in Ireland - an effort that seemed fruitless. But everything had changed when she met Jonathan.

In a moment of astonishing modernity, the nuns had allowed some of the sixth-formers to arrange a dance with a well-heeled boys' school.

"We're having a dance against Bridstock!" one of the girls had said excitedly, revealing her experience of contacts with other schools to date - which had all been netball or hockey matches.

Clare remembered with a smile how a nun had cornered Yvonne just as the coach for Bridstock was arriving, and tucked a lace mantilla into the front of her gorgeous long dress, which had apparently been considered too low and revealing. She had wondered how long it would stay there. Clare's own dress had been more modest - a simple cotton frock she was trying to pass off as a ball gown. Fashion had never been a strong suit for her family back in rural County Kerry.

It had been at that dance that she'd met Jonathan, and been swept off her feet by him. The nuns had slipped up in allowing the girls to choose the conveniently close Bridstock for their "away match", as it was a school of mixed religions, not just a Catholic school. And Jonathan was from the Irish Ascendancy, and Church of Ireland. They'd managed to arrange further meetings, and as Jonathan was truly smitten by this Kerry girl, he was keen to take responsibility when she fell pregnant, do the decent thing and marry her, despite the difference in religion. Clare had no particular interest in religion of any kind, so was quite unbothered by this.

Not so the two families! It was her family and his that had caused the rumpus. But with the speed necessitated by her condition, everyone had quietened down and the marriage had gone ahead, Clare being carried off to the family pile. Throughout this whirlwind romance and marriage she had completely abandoned her previous yearnings and plans. Bowled over by the novelty and fervour of being in love, her dreams were obliterated before the altar - as so many other girls' dreams had been. So she was back in Ireland again. Married. A mother. And no chance of university, debating societies, Bohemian friends, coffee bars, her long-imagined literary life.

She wound down the window and listened to a bird singing prettily in the gloom. She wondered if it was the famous nightingale, but reflected that it was more probably a robin.

She had done her time. Like so many others, she found marriage, however pleasant and comfortable - and Jonathan was kind - to be less sparkly than she'd anticipated. She'd given birth to Rollo, and a few years later to Marigold. She'd dedicated her life to her husband and her family, as the chatelaine of a large country house, entertaining endless streams of visiting businessmen and racehorse owners, managing the household.

She'd done her duty. As Peggy had done, till she could take no more of the mad poet she'd married.

Then Clare had escaped. She'd come back to England - not a million miles from her old stamping-ground - and put herself first, for the first time in so many years. And it was utterly enthralling!

She sighed loudly, closed the window against the evening damp, started the car again, turned on the headlights, and pointed herself home. She felt happier. She'd tapped into her driving force, her source, and this time nothing - absolutely nothing! - was going to stop her.

6

She arrived home late. It had been a long day, and as Clare got the coffee machine going she checked her messages.

"Hi Clary!" This was Nick. "They've got tennis courts at this swish hotel we're going to - just thought I'd mention it. Love to see you in a tiny tennis skirt ..." he laughed loudly before ringing off. Clare smiled - next week was going to be fun - deleted the message, and moved on to the next one.

"Clare? Um, it's Archie." Who the hell is Archie, she thought, as the message went on. "I wondered if you'd be free for dinner this week? Can you give me a call? We could talk about that feature we were discussing." Ah. She remembered Archie. A rather annoying little agent who was promoting some starlet or other. She found him quite creepy. No dinner. She'd ignore the call and deal with it if he came back again. Deleted.

"Hey Clare! Time for us to meet up. Let's have a drink. How about the Gluepot on Friday?" This was Paul, who'd been a long-time friend of Clare's since an assignment she was on where he was working for the BBC. He was always good for a laugh, a bit of gossip, and on occasion rather more, depending on how they both felt. She had no qualms about running several men-friends at once. It was her way of making sure she didn't get trapped by any one of them. Men could always play the field with impunity, and now she was able to control her fertility, she could play the same game. It was part of her plan to be independent as well as successful. She'd ring him tomorrow.

Next message: "Mum? I think you're going to have to talk to Marigold. Just sayin'. See ya!" Now what had got Rollo so concerned? All these veiled references to Marigold that were coming at her. Why didn't Marigold talk to her herself if she had a problem? She remembered the text she hadn't yet checked. This promised to be tiresome - something she really didn't have time to deal with right now. Her finger hovered over the delete button, then she put the phone down and turned back to her much-needed coffee.

She turned her thoughts to Echo's piece that she'd be starting work on the next day. This could be the making of her - a really important piece! It needed a lot of thought. But she was tired now. She threw together some bread, cheese and nectarines (nearly walnuts and toast!) and planned a lazy bath before bed. As she ate she thought back to when she'd stopped to ruminate in the car. Tabitha. She was the only one of that gang she was still in touch with, though she got occasional emails from Veronica, who was still friendly with Penny, who lived near Yvonne ... and so on. She'd love to see Tabitha again. She was so sensible. She blushed to think of how she'd been too busy of late to catch up with her. They'd got to know each other again, and got close after a twenty-year break, when Clare had arrived in England the previous year. And it had been just the right moment for Tabitha, who had been facing a crisis and was in dire need of help.

Clare had found it to be easy, seeing what Tabitha needed to do, giving her the help she needed to spur her on. She was trapped in a ghastly marriage, and quite blinded - by her honesty and feelings of indebtedness - to finding a solution. And Clare was so pleased to see the transformation in her friend, back to the happy, quiet but carefree girl she remembered.

I wonder if Tabitha would help ground me right now? she asked herself, then wondered why she felt uncomfortable, this fluttering in her stomach. Was it the nagging feeling that was steadily growing, that she should be attending to her daughter instead of chasing her own fame and fortune? Tabitha's always so down to earth, she thought. Then, "It's not too late to ring her," she announced to her empty flat. And so she did.

"Hey Clare! Lovely to hear from you!" Tabitha had said when she picked up the phone. Clare could hear the dogs pattering about on the vinyl floor of Tabitha's kitchen. "How's it all going?"

"Really good!" responded Clare with fervour. "I've just done the most amazing interview with Echo - you know, the woman who was lambasted in the papers for an unwise choice of a misbehaving boyfriend?"

"Oh, that Echo. Yes I know who you mean. What's she like? I often wonder what the real famous person is like, when they're not trying to be famous."

"Exactly! That's what my piece will be about. She's a nice woman, in fact. Likes paintings. Does some herself."

"Surprising - when you think of what we see on the screen. That sounds really interesting. You're a kind of investigative journalist, investigating people's hearts."

"Oh, I love that line! Think I'll pinch it," laughed Clare. "So long as I don't have to look too closely at my own! How about you?"

"Just getting everything ready for the new academic year. We've been auditioning madly, and got an interesting bunch of kids starting next week. What have you got there?" Tabitha's voice became muffled for a moment. "Let me have a look ... Oh, you're ok. Thank you. Where's your bear?"

Clare was used to these strange interruptions on calls with Tabitha. Her dogs were every bit as important as people to her and were accorded the same level of courtesy. It was part of what made her so guilelessly attractive.

"Sorry," Tabitha burst back onto the phone. "Cariad had something in her mouth. It was just a twig she'd brought in. I don't want crumbled stick all over the carpet - Maddie would go mad! - so I swapped it for one of her bears. Now where were we?"

Clare smiled as she thought of how her friend had landed on her feet, now with a perfect home, complete with housekeeper, and her new puppy - well, probably adolescent by now. "We've got such a lot to catch up on - I wonder, can I drop round? Tomorrow?"

"Can you make it after lunch?"

"Two?"

"That would be perfect! And bring some sensible shoes - the weather is so beautiful, you can join Esme and Cariad as we walk the grounds."

"I'll look forward to that," Clare said, completely genuinely. She was fond of Tabitha's dogs who behaved better than many people did. A stretch of the legs in beautiful scenery was just what she needed.

As she replaced the receiver she thought of the call she'd have to make to Rollo the next day. She needed to find out what was really going on with Marigold. The hints and veiled remarks were beginning to get to her, distracting her from her work. Now was the time she had to focus on her career, which was just beginning to take off. She needed to keep her slate clean and concentrate on that alone. She'd have to return Marigold's text too - but she was simply too tired now. Those calls could keep till the morning. The country air today, as well as all the driving, had made her tired. She finished her coffee and headed for her welcome bath and even more welcome bed.

7

Clare spent the morning working on her piece. The photos had come through and she was pleased with the effect Harriet had captured - of a strong but vulnerable person who thought deeply. Amongst them there was a charming image of Echo gazing from her French windows into the garden and the distant hills, looking fragrant and delicate and reflective, and very attractive. It must be something to do with angles and lighting - whatever it was Harriet was very good at it. She'd certainly book her again for her next gig.

As she listened to the recordings and got them transcribed, she thought about Linda, Echo's mother. She had kept out of the way mostly, but was clearly a rock in Echo's life. And she was there when Echo needed her. She'd left her home to stay with her daughter in her time of trial. Linda had recognised the vulnerable child in her flamboyant daughter, and dropped everything to be with her. She felt a sudden pang as she thought of Rollo's message from last night.

The phone rang. She was working so she let it go to message.

"Clare. Did you get the photos through from Harriet? I've seen them. They're stunning."

It was Joanne. Clare jumped up to grab the phone but she'd rung off already. She got that warm feeling that acclaim always gave her, and renewed her application to her task.

She didn't allow any more interruptions, and her focus resulted in a large part of the article being ready for first revision. She treated her pieces more like a major production than many journalists did - who were perhaps on the treadmill of churning pieces out fast, like a sausage factory. One of her friends actually called his pieces "sausages" during a particularly busy period when he was knocking out piece after piece. She preferred to think of her articles as delightfully decorated pieces of art, and gave them hours of loving care, with special attention to grip and flow.

Clare stretched as she tidied her table, and changed into "country gear" including those sensible shoes, before grabbing some lunch and setting off for Tabitha's place.

Tabitha lived in a charming summerhouse in the grounds of a big house belonging to a dotty old theatre fan. Lady Despont thought the sun shone from Tabitha's face, loved her dogs who were company for her own tetchy little lapdog, and gave Tabitha free run of the grounds, as well as the services of her housekeeper Maddie to clean the place. Tabs really had fallen on her feet, and Clare often felt quite choked up when she thought of the years that Tabitha had lost. Time could slip by so quickly when you didn't keep tight control over your life. They were firm friends again now, and she always looked forward to her visits to this haven of peace and calm, an island of countryside in a busy city.

So as she came up the familiar drive and her tyres crunched on the gravel, the summerhouse door opened and out flew two delighted dogs to greet her, with Tabitha standing in the doorway smiling. They greeted each other warmly, Clare loath to let go of Tabitha.

"Hey, what's this?" asked Tabitha, as she rounded up the dogs and invited them all inside.

"Oh, Tabitha," Clare shrugged as she slipped off her jacket. "Things are going so well that I feel in danger of getting bigger than my boots."

"Here, put that coat back on - let's start walking. Feeling the grass below your feet is going to help you think this out - whatever it is." Clare remembered with a rueful smile that walking the dogs was Tabitha's way of solving problems. Sometimes she walked for hours if the problem was large. Clare couldn't afford hours of walking today - she had an urgency about her that made her continually want to push herself. But then they couldn't walk too far anyway on this estate.

They set off through the magnificent grounds of Tabitha's home - the borrowed grounds. There were expanses of lawn, avenues of trees, all native deciduous ones which were still in full leaf and beginning to change to Autumn colours, varying from tree to tree. In places there were clumps of small flowering bushes, and Clare remembered seeing in the springtime swathes of daffodils and bluebells weaving through the birches and oaks. Tabitha waved to Joe Bucket, the indefatigable old gardener, who was always slowly working through the gardens. He gave her a gap-toothed smile and tipped his grimy old flat hat. They didn't stop to chat. He had a way of mangling the English language that was hard not to laugh at.

"I was talking to Joe the other day," Tabitha said quietly, as they walked on. "He said, 'I'm going to consecrate on that there Mongolia tree today', meaning he was going to concentrate on the Magnolia!" They laughed - fondly, not unkindly. They both worked with words, one way or another, and they liked the way Joe manipulated the English language in such an idiosyncratic way.

The dogs bounded around joyfully. Esme, the older of the two - and the one Tabitha had had such fun with in one of her drama productions for children, where the dog stole the show playing her part - knew she was off-duty and scurried about, nose to the ground. In contrast to the busy Springer Spaniel, Cariad, the larger though younger dog was of unknown parentage, with a solid body and a thick white coat. She was still a pup, and she danced and bounced along, always keeping an eye on Tabitha. Their simple joy was reassuring. Tabitha basked in it. And Clare realised how much she enjoyed it too. These two friends of Tabitha's were almost enough on their own to bring her back down to earth.

Clare related the events of her exciting day yesterday, emphasising her pride in how things were going.

"It sounds as if you're really achieving what you wanted when you arrived here last year," Tabitha responded. "So what's the problem?"

"Maybe it's just that after looking forward to this for so long I'm finding it hard to adjust? I dunno, Tabs. There's just something not quite right there. Something is grating. But I've no idea what."

"Remember this time last year?" asked Tabitha as she dished out a tiny piece of hot dog to each dog, as they wagged their whole bodies enthusiastically in front of her.

"How could I ever forget it!" laughed Clare.

"Can you remember how weird it all felt for me?" Tabitha turned to look at her friend. "After all those years of self-doubt. Being recognised? Valued?"

"Yes, I guess that's it. Though I never went through what you did ..." She accepted the leafy twig Esme had offered her, and plucked off the leaves one by one before tossing it rather inexpertly for the delighted dog, who hurtled after it as if her life depended on it. Cariad joined in the chase, but made no attempt to steal Esme's prize.

"Growing pains, perhaps," she added, as the twig was pressed into her hand again, now rather wetter. She handed it to Tabitha, who tossed it over her shoulder, saying "Enough, thanks, Esme."

"We've both changed so much in the last year," said Clare, turning to face Tabitha. "We've cast off our past lives and plunged into our new ones. In your case you had no choice, and now you're absolutely on course. But I've got a nagging feeling I may have thrown the baby out with the bathwater. That I'm betraying myself by cutting myself off from where I was."

They paused while Tabitha removed a length of cleavers from Cariad's bushy tail. "If you don't get them off straight away they knit themselves into matts and take ages later on .. There you go, Cariad!"

"Perhaps it's harder than I thought for this leopard to change her spots," Clare continued. "I do feel capable in my work - I know it's what I was born to do - and I'm happy enough playing around with the guys, nothing serious, just fun. But .. did you feel that perhaps everyone had made a mistake? That you were pulling the wool over their eyes and they'd suddenly see through you?"

"Oh yes," laughed Tabitha, "all the time! It took Timothy to take me aside and give me a bit of a talking-to to make me realise my value. I'm fortunate my boss believes in me! I think that's natural, Clare, especially after the way we were all so downtrodden for so many years at school."

"I was thinking about those days only yesterday," mused Clare. "I remembered a time when we were all discussing what we were going to be in life."

"One of our late-night dorm discussions?" asked Tabitha.

"Yes," laughed Clare easily, "where we put the world to rights. Bless us - such sweet little ingenues. And you know - apart from Veronica who famously wanted to be a nun but ended up with five children - we've most of us, eventually, got where we wanted to be. Certainly you and I have, albeit after a long, unplanned, diversion," she smiled. And Penny got her wealthy husband too. Yvonne, of course, is the big bold business-woman - none of us saw that coming!"

"Yes. It's interesting, isn't it?" agreed Tabitha. "Despite being babes in the wood, innocents, we knew even then what we really wanted. What was right for us. What would give us fulfilment and happiness." She paused to admire Cariad and Esme enjoying a fast chase, zigzag-ging through the silver birches behind the summerhouse as they had come full circle in their tour of the grounds. "Even if it took some of us so many years, so many wrong turnings, before we got there." She turned towards her house, adding quietly, "Deep down, we knew all along."

"But we just didn't listen to ourselves," said Clare thoughtfully.

They'd been out for nearly an hour, and were ready for a break and some refreshment, so Tabitha put the kettle on as they all arrived back in the house.

Clare threw herself onto the large comfy old sofa, kicked off her shoes and stretched out her long legs with a deep sigh.

"I love your little house, Tabitha. For me it's a haven. I can really relax here, not feel I should be doing something."

"I love it too," smiled Tabitha as she set out the mugs. "And I try to keep it a haven too. I do any admin work at the Academy, and only work on research and creative stuff here. So it's a warm and relaxing place, not contaminated with timetables or calendars!"

"I suppose that's something else we're guilty of. Trying to do too much. Over-achieving. I think it's bred into us, that we have to do more than men in order to warrant our place in the world."

"Ah now, that's a can of worms I'd rather leave closed," rejoined Tabitha, placing a steaming mug into Clare's hand. "Dogs - bed now," she addressed the two who had been padding about the room, and they went to their beds and lay down with a joint sigh equalling Clare's.

"That's a battle I don't really want to fight," she continued, sitting down at the other end of the squashy sofa, and tucking her feet up under her. "It's easier for us in the arts than for Yvonne in the business world," she added. "We woolly-minded liberals are more accepting of individuals, in the main," she smiled.

"That's true. And Joanne is happy enough with me. I hope. It's just something stirring inside me that feels out of balance. Something is making me feel guilty, and I resent it! You know, that sinking feeling in your stomach when you think you've done something wrong? Trouble is, I don't know what it is."

She took a long drink of her coffee, then said, "I lie. It's coming to the surface. Something to do with mothers and daughters, daughters and mothers. I had a basinful of them yesterday ..."

"Once this big piece is done perhaps you'll feel a bit differently?" asked Tabitha.

"I'm sure you're right. And I've got a lovely few days away coming up, with Nick. That'll cheer me up, definitely!"

The two friends fell to discussing Clare's current boyfriend strategy, which was firmly spreading her favours. She had no wish to settle down with any one person ever again. And after enjoying a chat about each other's friends and colleagues, they parted. Tabitha was due at the Academy for her evening students and Clare to drive back home after being escorted to her car by two whirling tails.

As always, Tabitha had put things back in perspective, even though they hadn't pinpointed the source of her unease, what was tingling inside her, nagging at her. She had work to do!

8

The next day was Friday, and after more work on her big piece, Clare met up with Paul for a drink after work. She'd got masses done: she'd even switched off her phone. "I can check the messages tomorrow. They can wait!" she said resolutely to herself, feeling proud of her dedication to her schedule. They were always fun, these occasional dates with Paul. He worked for BBC News, and they'd met on an assignment and had immediately hit it off. Clare blushed for a moment as she remembered that they'd actually cut short the hotel function they were both reporting on, in order to book a room and get to know each other rather better.

So that was how their relationship was. And it suited both of them just fine. Both unattached, they had an easy way with each other, and today they genuinely enjoyed the chat and banter over their toasted sandwiches. It was a useful friendship from the business point of view too. They could exchange information about their industry and the world in general. Journalists were always looking for new material!

And today Paul was probing for intel on the latest shenanigans of the current boy band sensation.

"Go on, you've got to know something," Paul urged her now, as he came back to the outdoor table with two halves of bitter. When in a pub, drink like you're in a pub, Clare always thought. Wine was for wine bars. And this pub was particularly interesting. Totally traditional inside with its dark wood decor, blackboards and horse brasses on the walls and pillars, externally it was also unchanged for many years. The glass signage all the way round the pub over the windows, painted with "The George" in traditional pub curly gilded lettering, the ornate pilasters round the doors and the character windows. These windows were one of the high points of the pub, as they sported Art Nouveau engraved lettering proclaiming the name of the pub as "The George" and "The Gluepot".

Clare had asked on her first visit there why it was so called.

"Ah, it's a lovely story!" Paul had explained to her. "It's the nearest pub to the Beeb, as you know, and in the days of the Henry Wood concerts - they're 'The BBC Proms' now - well in the early days when they were in the old Queen's Hall just near here, conductors would complain that getting their musicians back from the George after the interval was like getting flies out of a gluepot."

Clare smiled appreciatively at the story. "I don't know the Queen's Hall - where is it?"

"Bombed to oblivion, alas, at the beginning of the war. That's why they moved to the Albert Hall." Paul was a mine of information. "But of course the George is still always filled with BBC types, being just round the corner from Broadcasting House - Auntie's epicentre!" They laughed at his use of jargon - the BBC had famously been referred to as Auntie for a very long time.

So they sat outside the pub now on this early Autumn day, at a tiny metal table that just fitted on the narrow pavement as the busy street raced by them, with that particular city smell. Paul would frequently greet other patrons as they arrived or left, many being his colleagues, some giving meaningful glances at Clare, who was happy to meet them.

"Well," Paul prompted, as he polished off his sandwich, "What has this boyband been up to now? What's the gossip at Zenith?"

"I think you probably know more than I do, Paul," said Clare, making room between their plates for the tankards. "Not really my scene. But yes, there is something going on which may or may not involve drugs and ladies of the night."

"Sex, drugs, and rock and roll. Who'd a thought it? And where would we be in our profession without it?" laughed Paul. "Speaking of which … " his blue eyes looked intently into hers, "drink up."

As they travelled on the tube from The George to Paul's flat, Clare reflected as the train chuntered along too noisily for conversation, on how things had changed for her since she took her life into her own hands. She was now reliant on her own gifts to pay her way. And from a life of giving parties, watching racehorses, rearing children and lately doing her Open University degree, she was now happily feeling at home. She was on the tube, enjoying London - one of the greatest cities in the world - and with one of her boyfriends, with no ties. And yet, it was a mutually beneficial relationship they both had. They were in the same sort of industry, and could help each other. And it was interesting. It was fun. She was really enjoying herself: how things had changed! She banished the queasy feeling that started in her insides again. No, not now!

So they retired to Paul's flat a tube-ride away and enjoyed a few hours forgetting about the world and indulging their senses. It was a new experience for Clare, sex without attachment or duty, and she liked it. That was something that had always worked in her marriage with Jonathan, an enjoyable sex-life - and she had no wish to do without it entirely. She had not taken a vow of chastity when she left her marriage behind.

They'd stirred towards midnight for coffee and more food, and more setting the world to rights, before going back to bed again.

Clare noticed the pack of cigarettes on the bedside table.

"You don't smoke?" she said.

"No, but somebody else does," he said mysteriously.

"Who would that be?"

"You're not the only fish in the sea!" he replied. "They're queueing up for my favours," he smiled, drawing her closer.

"That's true enough," she said, "but I'm at the head of the queue right now." As they stopped talking, she had to accept she was playing the field, so he could play the field too. Clare enjoyed this light camaraderie, this lack of commitment - it suited her, so the last thing she needed was to feel possessive or jealous. She didn't know how long it would be before they would meet again - it was always informal and occasional - and she wanted to make the most of it while she was there.

When she awoke, Paul had already left as planned for his early assignment. Clare got up in leisurely fashion, showered and made herself coffee. She had glanced at the pack of cigarettes again as she dressed, with a pang of misgiving. Was she being a dog in the manger, not wanting to share what wasn't hers anyway? But now, drinking her coffee - Paul did have good coffee-making gear! - she dismissed such thoughts. She was a woman of the world, a woman on the move, a woman on the make. She was going to make sure her talents were seen by many, and at the same time enjoy a rich and varied life - without constraint. She congratulated herself as she thought of how well she was managing it all. So many people got tangled up in love and suffered for it. Tabitha had suffered for love in her strange triangle - she'd been in such a bad state when Clare had crashed into her life again a year ago and helped her see sense.

Clare smiled as she washed the coffee mug. She was good at this! Understanding people, helping them get their life together - it was a gift she seemed to have. Keeping her own life in order so she could make the most of it. She felt a shiver of pleasure as she said to herself, "I am in control!", threw her bag over her shoulder and slammed Paul's door behind her.

She took advantage of her lifted spirits, as she had to go back through the West End, to indulge in a little shopping. Some clothes that fitted her image - professional, casual ... and moneyed. She found a dress and a gorgeous pair of shoes for her hotel trip with Nick. She felt full of herself, on top of the world!

So it was already late morning when she made her way back to her flat, running through her mind all the things she was set to achieve today after her night off.

9

Climbing the staircase to her floor, Clare felt completely relaxed, at ease and ready to hit her work running. She was swinging her keys and her shopping bags and humming a tune from the disgraced boy band. She had never felt this independent and self-sufficient in her life! She'd always been looking after her original family, or mooning over Jonathan then marrying him and looking after her own family. She realised with surprise that her confinement in boarding school for all those years had actually afforded her a freedom of thought - despite the nuns. With nothing else to do and no-one else to look after, she'd been able to live in her intellect.

But as she reached the top of the stairs and rounded the corner towards her door she stopped short with a gasp.

Outside her door was a backpack and a crumpled person huddled against it. After her initial shock - What?! Was it a tramp? Was it dead? - the person moved and she realised to her horror that it was Marigold, looking so much older than her 19 years, dishevelled, tear-stained, desperate.

"Marigold!" Clare exclaimed. "What ...?"

Marigold turned a miserable face towards her mother and started sobbing.

"Oh my goodness," Clare dropped her bags to the ground and reached to help her up. "Come here - let's get you inside. How long have you been here? What's happened? Why aren't you in Dublin?" She fumbled with the key in the lock with a shaking hand, her other arm supporting Marigold, then got them both into the flat, which stood detached and still in the face of this drama. She turned to snatch up her bags and closed the door behind them.

Marigold sniffed and took the tissue Clare snatched from the box and passed to her. She blew and mopped and helplessly held out the tissue with a limp hand. Clare took it and handed her the box.

"Last night. I got here last night. The boat was delayed by the weather and the train took ages. I had no idea where you were. I didn't know what to do ..." she tailed off into tears again. Clare's stomach lurched with guilt as she remembered she'd been so enjoying herself with Paul that she'd turned her phone off - then never got round to checking her messages when she'd turned it on again.

"Come here," Clare reached out and took off Marigold's coat as if she were seven years old again. She eased her into an armchair, went over to the kitchen area to fill the kettle, then perched on the other chair, looking intently at her daughter. What on earth could have happened to get her in this state?

"I'm going to make you a hot drink and some food first of all, then you can tell me what's going on."

Marigold sniffed and started to weep again. She had never been pretty in the popular sense - though the older Clare got, the more she realised that all young girls are pretty just by virtue of being young and fresh - but she had charm, and now she was bereft of both looks and that charm. Her poor daughter!

Clare focussed on getting breakfast ready, giving Marigold time to recover a little. "Want to have a wash and brush-up?" she prompted, nodding to the bathroom. Marigold heaved herself from the chair and plodded towards the room. And was looking slightly more human when she came back into the living room.

She made short work of her coffee, but poked about with the toast and fruit. As Clare refilled the mugs, she said, "Can you tell me anything yet?"

After a long pause, "It's Tiernan." Marigold managed to get out, then went silent again, her eyes beginning to screw up.

"Tiernan?" encouraged Clare.

"He's left me," Marigold said with finality, her mouth working to suppress the tears.

"Oh darling, I'm sorry. He was a bit special, was he?"

Marigold's only reply was to cling to her mother, sobbing.

Clare was still nonplussed. Yes, she'd imagined Marigold had a boyfriend. But at nineteen, boyfriends came and went. Though her own first and only boyfriend hadn't left her, she reflected. But she had been pregnant. Now was a different age. Girls were different now. Why all the fuss over this one, who she hadn't even heard of?

"So ... why aren't you in Trinity? What made you come here?"

"I can't, I just can't ..." said Marigold between shudders and sobs.

"You're exhausted. Take another bite of toast and go to bed." Clare decided it was time to take charge. "The spare room's made up. Some of your things are still there from your last visit. We can talk about this later. Right now you need rest."

Getting her zombie-child eventually settled into bed, Clare went to her desk to start work. But she was shaken. And she was worried. This was an extreme reaction to a break-up. It seemed to have almost completely disabled her normally independent and capable daughter. Whatever was really going on? Her thoughts darkened - she dreaded to find out. And so she found it very hard to concentrate. Her carefully laid plan for her day had been smashed to smithereens by being dragged back into the role of mother. A role she'd managed for months now to keep in the background, as she forged her new life.

What was Marigold going to do? How long was she planning on staying? Did she have any plans at all? She'd talk to Rollo and find out what he knew - clearly his recent veiled hints had been pointing to this. Maybe Jonathan knew something? And what about her tutors? She couldn't lose her place at University!

She snapped the laptop shut. Her head was beginning to hurt. She couldn't work, but she needed to be doing. So she slipped on a jumper, grabbed her purse, phone, and keys, left a note by the kettle to say she was doing some food shopping and that Marigold wasn't to go anywhere, and left the flat.

Her first stop was a cafe, where she got hold of Rollo online - pretty surprising for this hour of the morning, night bird as he was.

"What is going on with Marigold?" she demanded of him.

He was fresh out of the shower and his hair was sticking to his forehead. "I told you something was up, Mum," he said.

"But what? What do you know? She's fetched up on my doorstep - literally - in a terrible state."

"Boyfriend trouble, I gather," he said, not hugely helpfully.

"But why the major meltdown?"

"Why do girls usually get in a state about a boyfriend?" Rollo asked enigmatically.

"No! Really? I haven't had a chance to ask her. So you think she's pregnant?"

"Well, it's a possibility, isn't it? That's all I know, Mum - got to give a lecture now - gotta go. Bye!" And the screen went black.

Next, she tried Jonathan. No reply. Hopeless. He'd be out in the yard, checking over the fitness of his entries for the next race. And he probably knew no more than she did, anyway.

She scrolled through her contacts list and her finger hovered over "Mummy". Peggy knew something. She'd been pestering her about Marigold in a meaningful way during her visit. What did she know? She suddenly realised she'd already been away for fifteen minutes and had yet to get the food. With a lurch of her stomach, she had a vision of Marigold leaving to go wandering again, put her phone away and set off for the supermarket at speed.

When she arrived home again, all was quiet. Marigold's coat was still thrown over the chair, so Clare's shoulders relaxed and she breathed easily as she quietly unpacked the shopping, screwed up the note still by the kettle, and started making coffee again.

She tried to still the anger rising in her chest. She had everything working perfectly. Why this massive spanner in the works from her daughter? And why did she feel so conflicted about this? Was it simply guilt - at her hedonism versus her daughter's grief? Or did she have a sneaky feeling that Marigold's dreams were about to be shattered, like hers had been?

Thinking of hedonism, she'd have to cancel the trip with Nick. She couldn't possibly leave her daughter in this state, and it didn't look as though her daughter would be leaving her any time soon. Her heart sank. Damn! Now that is *really* annoying, she thought, beginning to slam the groceries into the fridge and the cupboard as she seethed with silent fury. She had to shuffle the shelves about to accommodate provisions for two. She'd been so used to paddling her own canoe, only looking after herself, that having to rearrange her life to put someone else first again was grating on her. She thought she'd left that behind for the rest of her life. That she could devote herself to herself. And her work. It ripped through her chest, threatening to overwhelm her with frustration and anger.

There was no question in her mind that she had to look after Marigold. Her child had come to her for help. She couldn't refuse, nor would she - but she could certainly resent it! She banged the cupboard door shut. Those maternal feelings that had been driving her actions since she arrived home this morning were threatening to sweep over her. Love was trying to muscle in. She urgently squashed it down again while she concentrated on the practical issues. In truth, Clare was afraid her creative dream was being swept away again by her feelings of duty to others, leaving her thrashing about, panicking.

Later, when Marigold finally emerged from her room, to Clare's relief she looked a bit more as if she was in the land of the living. After picking about with the plate of food she'd been given, she was visibly less tense than earlier.

"Marigold," started Clare. "Marigold - I need to know what's going on. So I can help you."

Marigold sighed and stared at her hands.

"Are you pregnant?" asked her mother. She hadn't meant to blurt it out like that, but it was critical to know!

"No!" she said sharply. Then, "No, Mum, I'm not," she said, blushing - at last a little colour seeped into her wan cheeks.

"Well, that's a relief," said Clare, feeling the tension melting out of her shoulders. "Not that I'm blaming! You remember how old I was when I married your father and had you two. I'd never judge you for that!"

"Yes, but it's different," responded Marigold with verve. "I've got work to do! It's important to me! I want to complete my degree and do a Masters. I'm going to make a significant contribution to Irish Literature. Like Ampa did." It was cute alright, that she still used the name that toddler Rollo had used for their grandfather - a mispronunciation that had stuck. She toyed with the bread on her plate, maybe thinking of her over-achieving and brilliant grandfather. "I wouldn't be so stupid as to throw it all away by getting pregnant."

Clare flinched inwardly. She had thrown her own career away by getting pregnant, all those years ago. How 'stupid' had she been? She had to admire Marigold's determination ... but if Clare had not been 'so stupid' she'd never have had the joy of her two children. And joy it had certainly been. Who could resist their chubby knees and gurgling smiles; their sweet, innocent, laughter; their pure enjoyment of life? Teaching them, nurturing them. There was surely room for love as well as work in life? This last thought had slid into her mind, and she instantly pushed it out again. No! She knew that to do justice to her creativity she now had to focus wholeheartedly on it. That's how she could live up to her early expectations. That was how she would prove herself as a human being worthy of her place on the planet! Focus! And that's why she was keeping Paul and Nick at a comfortable arm's length. It was how her father had maintained his literary output all his life, by not watering it down with matters of the heart.

"So what has caused this meltdown, sweetie?" asked Clare, more gently.

"I thought he loved me," Marigold said bleakly, then dissolved into tears.

"Oh, here," Clare got up and sat on the arm of Marigold's chair, her arm round her shoulders, holding the bobbing head close to her chest. It didn't take much before her child's eyes were puffy and swollen again, her hands stirring her mass of dark curls into a mess. Clare reached out and put her hand on her forehead, the damp hair sticking to it: "You're feverish," she said. "Back to bed with you. I think the shock and journey have taken their toll." She stood up and took her daughter's arm, "Let's get you well first of all. We can talk about Trinity later. I think you may need to tell someone there what you're up to."

So she helped the shivering Marigold undress, tucked her into bed and kissed her hot face. "Sleep now," she said, closing the curtains and turning off the light before softly closing the door. She uttered a deep sigh of suppressed fury, and headed for her desk to try to work again. Was she going to have to choose between losing her job and losing her daughter?

10

Marigold's temperature ran high for another day. She could only be coaxed to eat a mouthful of food now and then. And when the fever passed, she seemed listless, depressed, hopeless. This was not Clare's feisty, charming girl!

Clare was busy all this time, arranging, re-arranging, trying to work. She cancelled the trip with Nick, who sounded as tetchy as she was, as he realised he only had a couple of days to find another partner for his junket.

"Ahh, sorry for your troubles, Clare, old thing," he said. "I wonder ..." he was clearly thinking who he could invite instead at this short notice.

"You'll find someone, you charmer you!" Clare laughed. She had no ownership over Nick, and that's how they liked it. "And if not, maybe you'll meet someone at the event who'll fit the bill?" She put the phone down with a sigh. She was disappointed not to be going, but there would be other times. Wouldn't there?

Her call from Joanne was rather more tense.

"Where's this piece?" demanded her editor, without preamble. Her day was evidently not going well.

"Joanne. I've got a bit of a family crisis," Clare said, sounding so lame.

"I need it." Joanne said curtly. The magazine goes to bed next Tuesday. I need it by ... Saturday night. Ok?"

Clare looked at her screen with the only partly-finished piece open on it. "Right," she said, with an air of confidence she didn't feel, "You'll have it by then."

She had to get herself organised! Her life had been so carefully managed, everything in its place, like a well-oiled machine. Now it was all asunder and she didn't like the feeling of helplessness it engendered.

She thought of the call she'd had from Jonathan early this morning. Clare could hear a horse whinnying in the background. He must have been in his office in the yard, back from the gallops. She could picture him at his desk at her old home, as she heard the sounds of buckets and barrows, busy stable lads shouting to each other in their strong local accents - that soft lilt peculiar to County Meath - and the clopping of horses along the paths. For a moment she savoured the country, horsey, smells in her imagination.

"What's going on, Clare?" he asked. "Rollo tells me Marigold's left Trinity. Is this true?"

Clare had given him as much information as she had herself - which wasn't much. She'd been on to Marigold's tutor to explain that she was ill. The tutor was relieved to hear that his star student would be back again soon. "Such an addition to the department," he said, "A good mind." Clare sighed: university-speak.

"She can stay here till she perks up a bit," she told Jonathan. "then I'll pack her off to Dublin again. I don't know why she's taken this so hard." A horse snorted loudly as it passed Jonathan's office window.

"Is she in trouble?" asked Jonathan, using that old-fashioned phrase.

"No, she's not. Swears she isn't."

"Maybe her work was getting on top of her and this Tiernan fellow was the last straw. She's normally so level-headed."

"She takes after you!" Clare smiled as she thought of her capable, business-minded husband.

"Let me know what happens," he said, as he rang off.

She saw ever more clearly with each day that it was up to her alone to deal with this crisis. She was firmly back in the driving seat she had so recently escaped - the organiser of family things, whether outings or crises. She wondered whether she should organise some sort of counselling for Marigold. Perhaps a bit later ... For now she had to focus firmly on her piece. It was not going to write itself!

The pleasure was in danger of seeping out of the project now. She had to keep in mind the day she'd visited Echo, the whimsical side of her character, her ability to keep that alive in the teeth of a brash pop career - her fragility, her mother's support.

Her mother's support! She picked up the phone again and dialled Peggy.

"Mum, you were right. I don't know how you knew, but Marigold's having a crisis. She's landed here in a sorry state."

"Oh no! What's happened?" asked Peggy urgently.

"Boyfriend trouble, it seems. This guy Tiernan has left her and she's in bits over it."

"Poor girl. What's made her take it so badly, I wonder? She's not ...?" she tailed off.

"No. Swears not."

"But she needs huge support now," Peggy added. "She's at a vulnerable age. She has to know we're there for her."

There was a pause. "When I was in trouble at that age, you weren't there for me," said Clare bluntly.

Those had been torrid times. Being in her last term at school, her bump beginning to show. Trying to make excuses for why she felt sick all the time. The only person she'd told was her friend Tabitha. She'd confided in her one night when she couldn't bear being alone with her secret any more. Tabitha had been so supportive! It had made such a difference, despite Tabitha having no experience at all of this kind of thing. "You *have* to tell your parents," she'd said. "You have to." Clare knew how disapproving her father would be. The shame of having a daughter up the duff, his academic colleagues laughing at him, making ribald jokes at his expense. But she knew Tabitha was right. There was only so long she could keep it secret anyway. Maybe her mother would protect her from her father's wrath. Surely she would?

But she hadn't. Peggy had gone along with Michael in their shock and condemnation. She'd meekly toed the family line. At least they had both been in favour when Jonathan asked her to marry him. "She'll be off our hands in haste, and the young man can pay for his mistake at leisure," as she'd painfully overheard her father saying one evening. And despite 'kicking with the other foot', he was a wealthy land-owner, and a catch.

"You didn't look after me when things went wrong," she said again, accusingly, into the silence.

"And it's to my eternal shame." Peggy sighed. "I was in thrall to your father. He owned me. Even after I'd left him years before. He said, 'She's made her bed, let her lie on it'."

Clare stayed silent.

"And in any case, your Jonathan was quite a prize. 'Let her get on with it,' said Michael, 'She'll never make much of herself otherwise.'" Peggy paused.

"So ... I regret to say ... I went along with your father. I should not have done that. I should have ignored his rantings and helped you."

This was the first time they'd ever talked of this time, and Clare found her throat hurting.

"Don't let's perpetuate this. Don't let it happen again for another child. We need to look after her. She needs to know we will always back her."

"Mum, I can't be doing this. I'm really, really busy. Don't you see, I've got a great chance to make my mark here! This piece - it could be the making of me."

"I've learnt a lot down the years," said Peggy slowly after a pause. "I saw how alone your father was at the end. He'd spurned the very people who could have given him the most comfort. After I left with all of you children, he had nobody who really cared. Lots of sycophants, sure, but no-one who really knew him. I even offered him to live in our house - make a separate flat for him, so he could see all of you all the time. But he preferred his career."

"I did try to reach him .." said Clare, "but he was always so aloof."

"I can tell you now," said Peggy, pulling the mother card again and speaking *ex cathedra* - from the throne of her official mother position - "If you can't balance your work and the people who are important to you, you're going to be a very unhappy person."

The silence was at Clare's end now, and into that silence Peggy said quietly, "Let me know as soon as she's able to talk to me. I'd offer to come down and stay with you so you can work and I mind my granddaughter. But I know how fiercely independent she is ... usually. I think I should wait till she wants to tell me. I don't want to be the interfering granny. Get her to ring, when she's ready."

"Ok, Ma," said Clare disconsolately. "Bye."

11

Marigold got up early the next morning and showered. This was a good sign, thought Clare. She must be feeling a bit better. Not "better", but "betterer", as she'd say as a young child. Clare was relieved to see her movements returning to usual - she was sparkier, not dragging herself about. But she was surprised when Marigold announced that she was going out.

"Darling, you aren't ready, are you?" she asked with concern.

"I won't be too long. I feel … I just feel the need to get out, get some fresh air, walk a bit."

"What money have you?"

Marigold looked up under her lowered lashes. "I'm a student, Mum, remember? I had to shell out for the boat and train fares …"

"Here." Clare rummaged in her purse and found some notes. "If you suddenly go floppy, get a taxi back." She paused, then stuffed a couple more notes into Marigold's hand. "I don't want you to collapse in the street. You've hardly eaten for days." And so saying, she started getting breakfast things out of the cupboards and fridge.

She was pleased to see Marigold eating, albeit not much. And she was pleased to see her looking pinker, healthier. She was her mother, and she did care. But how much was her pleasure coloured by her eagerness to have her place to herself again, get on with her ordered life again?

"Mum, I do appreciate you looking after me," said Marigold, turning her face to her as she pushed her plate away, most of the food having been eaten. "I had to get away. I didn't know where to go. Then I thought of you."

"Sure and where else would you go?" Clare heard herself saying. "You just need to step back for a bit, then you'll be back to your old self in no time." She fervently hoped this was so, though she did genuinely mean it.

Marigold leant forward and gave Clare a kiss on the cheek. "See you later," she said, scooping the money off the table, stuffing it into her pocket, and shouldering her bag. She gave a brittle smile as she turned to the door.

"Don't be too long!" Clare called to her as the door closed behind her.

Clare cleared up the table and set to work. She put Marigold out of her mind and focussed on what she had to get done. She hated running close to deadlines, the panic bubbling just below the surface, and she was keen to get 'Echo' done and dusted, and off to Joanne.

Said Editor rang during the morning. "Look Clare, sorry about yesterday. Three people are off with flu, including Tina." Tina was Joanne's amazing Admin, who more or less kept the whole of Zenith Publishing going single-handed.

"Oh no! It's hard to imagine Zenith without Tina at the helm." Clare sympathised, glad to be speaking to a more accessible Joanne today.

"Who're ya telling?" laughed Joanne shortly. "Well, we had to juggle some pieces for this month's issue because of it. I knew you were working hard on 'Echo' so I reckoned I could count on you to fill the gap."

"It's ok, Joanne, I'm happy to. You know you can always depend on me! I'm almost done anyway," Clare crossed her fingers as she said this, with a quick glance at the screen displaying her paltry word-count. "It's going to be a great piece, though I say it myself! I found Echo fascinating - much more interesting than I'd imagined from her public persona."

"I'll look forward to seeing it," said Joanne. "And Clare - you said you had a crisis: is there anything I can do?"

"Oh no, it's fine, thank you Joanne," she said, unaccustomed to this gesture from her editor. "Just teenager trouble," she laughed lightly, feeling a stab of disloyalty as she did. "It was all a bit fraught yesterday, but things will be back to normal in no time."

So she'd got absorbed in her work - feeling a lot happier and more relaxed - and was churning out words when she suddenly realised that it was nearly lunchtime and there was no sign of Marigold. Where could she be? The anxiety gripped her. She had visions of her daughter on a hospital trolley, nursing staff around her with long faces. She snapped herself out of these ridiculous thoughts - but how ridiculous were they? Marigold still hadn't talked to her. Hadn't explained why she was so very upset. She thought about what Jonathan had said, and hoped this collapse didn't signify a bigger problem, of mental breakdown.

Marigold had always been such a sunny child. Clare saw her in her mind's eye now, standing before her in her winter coat and that fair-isle beret Peggy had made for her, her wellies mud-caked, her bare knees pink with the cold. "We're making a tree-house for the fairies!" she said with excitement, pointing to a heap of old branches propped up against a big beech tree, Rollo crawling about inside them. Bath-time would have been fun that night, Clare smiled to herself now. "It's going to be a tree-house, only on the ground," Marigold had added, so that Spencer and Trudie can come in with us." Clare smiled as she remembered the devotion Marigold had long had to her pets. They were always included or at least allowed for in her games, and she mothered them mercilessly, making elaborate beds and houses for them in her room. While Spencer the dog preferred the floor, Marigold made a wobbly structure out of cardboard boxes for Trudie that she called the Cat Flats, with doors and windows cut out, and soft toys and blankets in every storey.

Such happy days. Endless days. They all merged into one long lightness of heart. Clare had loved her children when they were small and around all the time. It was a time of suspended animation. The world stopped spinning while Clare spent time with her little ones. A time out from reality. It was Jonathan who had insisted on them going to boarding school once they hit double figures, as he had done, as was the norm in his family. Clare was torn between her loss and the possible gains for the children. She had benefitted from being away at school, after all - albeit at a later age - after so long not being allowed to go to school at all by her eccentric father. Maybe Rollo and Marigold would make firm, lifelong, friendships there - as she had done with Tabitha. But her life was empty without them at home. Long months of silence in the house, no-one to tend, feed, and clear up after. That was when she'd started the Open University degree. She suddenly saw her opportunity to reclaim her early promise and do something for herself. This could be her moment! With no-one else to focus on but herself. Jonathan was occupied with his racing stable and the estate - always busy, always some issue to deal with, some race meet coming up, some function to attend. And the children were off developing themselves, becoming adults. So she immersed herself in her studies. At last, after all those 'years off', she could devote herself single-mindedly to her calling.

And she loved it! She was back to writing fluently again in no time, feasting her mind on the glories of literature, and moulding everything she learned into her own style, which gradually formed itself. It was strange to have the kitchen table covered with books, laptop, and papers, after so many years of flour and pastry, biscuit-cutters, plastic bricks, chemistry experiments - that burnt patch had never really been mended properly - but it was now her space. She dove into it each morning while Jonathan was on the gallops, and was pleased to find that she could work for hours on end, keen and eager for more.

And when she'd gone to the summer schools that were part of the distance-learning course, she was able to stay up half the night talking about writing with her newfound colleagues. She was living that early dream, of going to university. Admittedly it was fifteen years later than she'd planned, but it had happened! And this independence of mind naturally led to her wanting more. Jonathan was entirely absorbed and content with his work, and their conversation had become very samey and lacklustre. So neither of them were surprised when, once the children were both set on going to university, Clare decided to leave the family mansion and move to England, back to the city where she had lived with her mother all those years ago, and make her way as a journalist.

The children were surprised too, rather than shocked. They were both so wrapped up in their own lives, their interests, and their friends, that it didn't worry them too much. Rollo was the first to notice the big plus of having a base in England to do his university interviews from. He had long set his heart on one of the ancient English Universities for his studies, while Marigold was firmly rooted in Ireland.

But it was Marigold who had said one day, "Daddy will be able to spend as much time as he likes with Aisling now." Clare felt a great jolt through her body. How had she completely missed this? Aisling was the very capable trainer who had worked with Jonathan for years. Jonathan and Aisling? She'd had no idea! She had been so involved in her studies that she had completely failed to notice.

So her big bid for freedom was a bit of a damp squib after all. Her parting from Jonathan had been not only amicable, but welcomed by both of them. Having been thrown together so young and accepted their responsibilities, they knew they had performed their tasks well. Jonathan had been an attentive husband and plentiful provider, while Clare had reared the family and made a wonderful home for them all, while supporting Jonathan's work with her entertaining. It had been a good chapter - but they both wanted to turn the page now. They'd done what they felt they had to do for their children, and were now free to indulge themselves. Clare had no special person in mind as a partner, but she'd noticed stirrings when she was at the summer schools, and the prospect of being able to play the field again, after such adventures being stopped when she was so young, was quite enthralling.

She and Jonathan had gone their separate ways without misgivings. He was generous in ensuring that she had enough money to get by on till she could fulfil her dream of earning for herself. Clare was so glad that that happened surprisingly fast, so she didn't have to feel reliant on him. And they were both united in wanting the best for Rollo and Marigold, and spoke to each other regularly about finances and plans. Money had never been an issue for Jonathan. While the outgoings on the estate were massive, the income kept comfortably ahead of them, and when the children needed help, they got it.

A key turned in the lock of the front door, and she snapped back to the present and jumped up - for the moment wondering who it was breaking in.

"Marigold!" she exclaimed, "Are you ok? You've been ages! Where have you been?"

"Oh, here and there," said Marigold enigmatically. "I'm feeling much better, Mum. I'm starving."

This was always music to a mother's ears, so they went to the kitchen and chose what they wanted to eat. And it was during lunch that at last Marigold unburdened herself to her mother.

"Tell me about Tiernan," Clare had said, after their early hunger was assuaged and they slowed down their eating. "What was special about him that he captured your heart so?"

Marigold sighed, and told a long and convoluted story of dates, meetings, promises, arguments, and heartbreak. She smiled distantly as she talked of the little gifts he brought her - poems written just for her.

"Is he a good poet?" asked Clare quietly, not wanting to break the flow.

"Pretty good. Yes. But I see that Ampa was part of my attraction for him, now I think about it."

Clare winced at this realisation of Marigold's. Painful! To think the boyfriend was using her to learn more about her grandfather!

"I really thought Tiernan loved me," she ended up. "I really thought he did," she gazed out of the window, looking over the rooftops to the clouds scudding by in the autumn sky. Her eyes filled with tears again - so many tears! "But I'll get over it, I suppose." She turned those watery eyes back to her food, with a shrug of her shoulders.

"Time is a great healer," said her mother now. "And you are so good at what you do. You were top of your year last year. Going to do that again this year?"

"I will, but it'll only be by the skin of my teeth. My work fell away badly in the summer term ... Tiernan, you know. But I had enough marks stacked up to stay at the top. This year will be different! I absolutely love Irish and the magic and mystery of its literature. And yes, I want to follow in Ampa's footsteps and help to keep it alive, vibrant - understood as it should be. The language is intertwined with the soul of Ireland, the Irish people - even the diaspora. They depend on the permanence of their language and traditions. I want to ensure its continuance."

"Well, that's quite a speech! And quite a goal. I love that you're so passionate, Marigold. And having something that you alone can do is so important. If you feel this strongly about what you do, then go for it, girl!" Clare enthused. "If you have gifts, you have a right - a duty! - to use them."

Marigold gazed back at her in silence, her big brown eyes opening to this thought.

"I think you should rest now," said Clare, as she stood to clear the table. "Do you want to go to bed for a nap, or ... you could rest on the sofa and watch a film on your laptop - but have you got earphones? I need to carry on working. I'm on a deadline."

Marigold acquiesced. "Yes, I feel exhausted now. I'll rest on my bed and watch a film. Good idea."

She smiled shyly at her mother. "And ... can I stay here a bit longer, Mum?" she said, as she twirled her fingers through the crumbs on her plate. "I don't feel strong enough to go back yet. It's all too raw."

"Course," said Clare. She wanted to do her best for her daughter, at the same time hating the intrusion. "You need time to get better. Here is where you need to be."

There. She'd said it. She'd sealed her fate for the next ... who knew how long? Marigold looked a lot better today, but she was still very fragile. She could relapse and be here for weeks. The award would float out of the window, out of Clare's grasp. Her heart lurched. And she quieted it.

12

"I'm having a training session with Melanie and the dogs tomorrow morning." Clare could hear Tabitha flipping the pages of her diary as the scrunching noises suggested she was nestling the phone under her ear. "Here! Why don't you come over at twelve and we can all have lunch together?"

"Perfect!" said Clare, feeling calmer already. She'd been worrying about her deadlines and her daughter all night, and she knew she needed the rock solid influence of Tabitha - and she was pleased she'd be getting Melanie into the bargain. She'd met Melanie when she'd been working with Tabitha to get her dog Esme ready for a part in one of the kids' drama school productions. She was different from what Clare had always imagined dog trainers to be. She was kind, thoughtful, had studied her subject at University level - a surprise in itself to Clare, that you even could study dog behaviour - and, she never laid a finger on a dog, except to love them. This last was why Tabitha was so keen on working with her, and it was rubbing off on Clare too. She found that just talking to her was an education in itself! For Melanie had found early on that you could have all the knowledge in the world about how dogs behaved, but you'd get nowhere if you couldn't bring the owner with you. So her practical knowledge of human psychology was almost as solid as her understanding of dog behaviour. There were plenty of parallels with the way people behaved with each other too, which fascinated Clare. She really was worth a piece, she thought ... must put it to Joanne.

Though Melanie was nearer to Marigold's age than her own, Clare had hit it off with her as soon as they'd met and they always got on well, and Melanie had been such a support to Tabitha in her dark night a year ago. She had a cooling effect, practical, and easy-going - just what Clare was lacking at the moment!

"I need another perspective on all this," Clare added. She needed to get things in proportion again.

"All what, Clare?"

"Ah, I'll tell you tomorrow. See you at noon." And she rang off.

It was twice in a week now that her car had crunched onto Tabitha's gravel drive (why was it the noisiest drive ever? Must be the kind of stones, she thought. She couldn't remember the sweeping drive at Brownestown sounding like this.) And she got her usual ecstatic greeting from Esme and Cariad. As she stepped from the car surrounded by a flurry of tails, she realised how much this simple greeting meant to her - how the dogs' openness with someone they knew and their undiluted pleasure at seeing them contrasted with her own complex thoughts.

"Hey!" she called out, as she noticed there appeared to be more than two dogs whirling round her legs, "More dogs, Tabitha?"

"Rhys!" called Melanie, appearing in the doorway, explaining the mystery - and one of the tails detached itself from the group as her collie shot back to her side, where Clare saw another dog close beside her, not joining in the party.

"Hi Melanie! I didn't recognise Rhys for a moment in all the excitement. Hello Heidi," she said quietly as she walked toward the house. She'd learnt that Heidi was a shy dog and did better without a direct gaze or super-friendly greetings. "Where's Tabitha?"

"She's just getting the lunch together," said Melanie, leaning forward to give Clare a hug, her short mop of red curls tickling Clare's face. "You working too hard as usual?" she asked, "You feel all tense."

"Ah, *there's* a tale," Clare gave a rueful smile. "I've got a lot on my plate at the moment. I'll tell you about it - I'm hoping you two sensible people will inject some calm into my life again." Her carefully-regulated life was all asunder. She thought of the phone calls she hadn't made this morning, the text from Nick she hadn't been able to face replying to, the icy fingers that gripped her when she thought of her next call to Joanne.

"Well, knowing you, Clare, you wouldn't want it too calm!" They laughed as they went in, Tabitha drying her hands and greeting Clare with the same warmth. They know I need them, thought Clare, as she returned Tabitha's hug. How lucky I am to have such reliable friends. Peggy saw her as standing alone, but she wasn't. She had these special people, with whom she had no ties other than affection and mutual respect.

"So?" asked Tabitha, after they'd chatted for a while over a pleasant meal. "What's up, friend?"

Clare told them the whole story, from the wonderful opportunity to win an award, finding her desperate daughter on her doorstep, to cancelling her trip with Nick, nearly missing her deadline, her mother guilt-tripping her, and trying to cope with her completely disrupted life.

They listened without interrupting.

"Wow," breathed Melanie. "You've got everything happening at once! Your possible career breakthrough, and your daughter in crisis."

"The two big things in your life coming up against each other," added Tabitha perceptively. "Your work and your family."

Clare returned Tabitha's gaze as she marvelled at her cool perspicacity, her ability to get to the nub of the problem.

"It's thrown me into turmoil, alright." She gave a short laugh and started fiddling with the knife on her plate. "You see, I've always wanted to be a creative artist, a writer. Then my life was hijacked for twenty years while I had the children. That's another story, really. I don't blame them, of course! It was my choice. But I've always felt that if I don't create, I'm failing. What will I have to show for my life? And now, just as I've got things moving in the right direction, Marigold chucks a spanner in the works."

"I'm sure she's not doing it on purpose," said Melanie. "The poor kid seems to be in a state?"

"Oh no, it's not that. Yes, she really is in a state, though she's a little bit more stable every day, thank goodness. She'll get better and things will go back to normal." She looked up at Melanie, "But it's how it makes me *feel* that's shaken me. I feel I can't escape from motherhood, service to others, long enough to pursue my art."

"You're getting known for writing sensitive pieces - penetrative, thought-provoking pieces about people, aren't you," said Tabitha, apparently going off at a tangent. "Is that what this award is about?"

"It's called the Journalism Social Impact Award, and yes, that's what I do! My piece about you started the ball rolling, Tabitha! Showing the real person behind the public image. People loved that piece. Showing that an achiever can still be quiet and humble. It's influenced what my Editor sends my way."

"But you couldn't write those pieces if you didn't have empathy for the subjects. It's the fact that you've loved, you've cared for others, that brings that to your work, isn't that so?" said Tabitha, quietly.

"Perhaps if you'd gone straight into your writing career," chipped in Melanie, "instead of being diverted into motherhood, you wouldn't have the depth of feeling and experience that you have. You wouldn't be *you*?"

Clare smiled appreciatively at Melanie. "I think I always felt destined for greater things. Having such a famous father to follow, I suppose. Anyone can have children - oh Tabitha, I'm sorry ..." she leaned forward anxiously, her hand held up in peace.

"Don't worry, I know what you mean," Tabitha reassured her. Tabitha, who had been childless not by choice, and had suffered greatly because of it, reached out and gave Clare's raised hand a squeeze. "Isn't producing and rearing two wonderful children a creative act in itself? Isn't that sufficient legacy?"

"No." Clare had abandoned annoying them with the knife and picked up her mug and gazed into it. "Yeah, they're great kids - well, most of the time they are! But it's not enough. There's this drive within me. And I feel that every time I start getting somewhere with it, it gets derailed. I haven't written the Magnum Opus yet. I haven't done all those things that I wanted to do so many years ago. I'm not yet forty, but I can hear the clock ticking! I know I've got this yearning to create in me, and if I don't get my creativity out there then I've failed. And family commitments are always a big roadblock. They interfere."

Tabitha leaned forward and put her mug down on the floor. "I used to keep my life in separate compartments." She gave Clare a crooked smile. "Do you remember, Clare?" Clare nodded vigorously. "And when one thing went wrong it had a catastrophic effect on all the other things."

"It sure did!" said Clare. "You were a mess, to be honest." Clare thought back to the torrid times when she'd helped her friend see a way forward out of her confusion of failing marriage, an adoring but ambition-less lover, her passion project that was failing to grow as it should, and the misbeliefs and major disasters she encountered along the way.

Tabitha smiled and nodded, now so much wiser. "You can't keep them separate. You have to make them all work together. Maybe I wouldn't have gone so far down the wrong track if I'd kept things balanced? You see, I had different levels of tolerance for each area. Different levels of integrity. I took each category - a relationship, or work - and focussed on it in isolation, without relating it to anything else. It's not surprising that when one pillar crumbled the whole edifice collapsed!"

Clare stiffened, her mug halfway to her mouth. Then she slowly lowered it to the table again. This truth had surely hit her amidships!

There was a pause while they all watched Cariad start chasing a bunny in her sleep, with paddling paws, muffled squeaks, growls and tiny woofs. As they smiled at this performance, she gave a mighty stretch, sighed, and reverted to deep sleep again.

"Know what I think?" said Melanie, who'd been sitting back, thinking, for a while, pensively twirling her fingers round Heidi's ear. "I think we're still struggling to adjust to a male world. This is a male thing, this need for achievement. As Tabitha said, what more important thing can you do than carrying, giving birth to, and rearing the next generation to look after us? You see, men couldn't do that - they had to find something different. So they made their working achievements a sign of their success. That's why women have been so undervalued for so long."

She went on, "I'm a sort of cultural savage. I know nothing about all this, but isn't it so, that famous artists are all *men* - like composers and writers and Shakespeare and so on - aren't they all men?"

Tabitha jumped in, "Well certainly there are more men in art in history, and there could be lots of reasons for this. Partly it's because women weren't educated for ages. They didn't even have their own name. They didn't own anything - they were slaves, owned by their father or husband. But also they didn't have the same sort of upbringing - like, early on monks learned music as the children of the cloister, and how to read and write and draw. Girls didn't get those opportunities. They weren't expected to do anything for themselves - just serve the men in the household." She was in full flow now, animated by one of her favourite subjects.

"Then later, there were women writers who used men's names so that they'd get the chance of being published. And painters? Well, I guess men had the freedom to go off painting all day long, or even own a studio with apprentices, working for rich patrons. Back in the day, men didn't have to change nappies and worry about getting homework done, doing the ironing, getting the rent paid, hefting in the coal, getting dinner on the table. It's much more equal now. Women's education is much better and they have many more rights than they used to have. Thank goodness! Otherwise where would we three be? We've all benefitted from further education of one kind or another.

"And we *are* creative!" Tabitha concluded as she spread her arms out. "Look at us! But you don't have to put your love on hold while you create. We can do both!"

Clare remained silent, as she absorbed this. She looked up to hear Melanie speaking.

"That's where we score. We can do both. We don't have to measure our achievements against the masculine standard. Now I know things are changing! Lots more men are getting so much more involved in daily life with their families." She was leaning forward in her seat, animated, her dog now dozing by her feet. "Women are showing that they can contribute just as much to the world as men have, traditionally - in business, art, medicine, politics. People are feeling more able to express themselves in the way that suits them best. Look at my father - he's the oldest of old-fashioned men in his upbringing. But when my mother died he thought that making the best of me was more important than moving further in his career, and he focussed on that. But it brought out the feminine side of him, and he found that that balance made him better in his business dealings too. Does that make sense?"

"Ye-e-e-s," said Clare slowly, "I think I see what you're getting at."

What they were saying ran counter to everything she'd always thought. But everything she'd always thought was not working for her! Her friends seemed to be streets ahead of her in navigating this world they all lived in.

"Even I want to have a family one day," Melanie continued. "I'd love to have children. Oh, don't worry, I won't think of them as dog-substitutes!" They all laughed and enjoyed the lightening of the mood.

Tabitha leaned forward. "You're thinking very black and white, Clare. That you have to have one or the other. You're an amazing woman, but you don't have to be Superwoman. Why not have room for both?"

"I've been spoilt," sighed Clare as she leant back into the squashy, comforting, sofa. "I've got the kids off to university - got them started in their careers. And focussed on myself. I thought that once in motion, they'd continue. I enjoy hearing their news, but ... at a distance. I thought my time had come. When I could focus on what *I* wanted to do. I don't really know where this came from, that I could only do one or the other?" She bit her lip. She was lying! Of course she knew. It was what her father had inculcated into her from an early age. It was embedded in her. It was time she recognised that a central plank of her belief system had been nailed in place by someone else. It had not been chosen by her.

"We all like to have our own space," Melanie said. "I know I do! How long is Marigold going to be with you?"

"And how much attention does she need?" added Tabitha. "I mean, you're able to get away today?"

"She's taken to going out for long walks round the city in the mornings. Head-clearing, she says. She's still very vulnerable, and still breaks down in tears regularly. I couldn't send her away like this."

"Could someone else help? How about her father? Or your mother?"

"I could ask Jonathan, I suppose. I'm not sure how well Marigold gets on with Aisling, though. And Peggy is desperate to help, but wants the request to come from Marigold. No, it's down to me. And, you know, I *can* manage the practical side of it. I'm able to work at home for the moment, parcel out my time so that I can still get things done. It's the feelings it's all dredged up that have hit me amidships."

She uncrossed her legs and shifted forward in the chair again.

"When I was a girl I was always seeking love."

"Weren't we all!" rejoined Tabitha, pouring herself some more coffee after the others waved away the offered jug. "Remember all that heartache we talked of endlessly at school - how we longed to experience a broken heart, as books and films seemed to indicate this was the only way to understand love?"

Clare smiled at the memory, and wondered for a moment if this is what Marigold believed too, whether she'd swallowed the popular cultural view of love. Then she continued, "Well, when I found love, I felt trapped. I felt I was denying my truth. My energy went into looking after Jonathan and his business, and in rearing my children the best I could. Only when they left home did I feel able to pursue my dreams. That's where I felt that I would really find happiness. Fulfilment."

"You're doing it again," said Melanie. "You're doing this one-or-the-other thing."

Clare nodded and paused. "But I seem to be chasing a chimera. I'm always thinking, 'when I get this piece accepted I'll have arrived,' or 'when I can disconnect from a relationship with ease, I'll know I've achieved independence'. I seem to be always waiting for the next thing in order to feel good."

"My Dad says that that's the trouble with loads of people - they're living in the future when things will be just right. Or, of course, they're living in the past when they thought they had everything perfect! He says that's what made him realise what was important when Mum died. She was history, the future was uncertain - but he had me now, and that was what he put his mind to," said Melanie.

Clare gazed at Melanie. She was younger than the rest of them, but seemed to have it very well together.

"I do what I can every day to feel satisfied, happy," added Tabitha, after a pause to assimilate Melanie's words. "Then I take each day as it comes. The future will take care of itself. But you have to set it up right, now."

"So it's a double-whammy," chipped in Melanie. "You think you can only achieve in life if you focus on your art alone, and you're putting your happiness on hold till ... till what? Till you're famous? How famous? Rich? How rich? How will you know when you've got there?"

Clare held up her hand to interrupt Melanie. "Do you know, I have no idea. I'd never looked at it that way. I just feel that I have to forge forward towards ... success. But you're so right! How *will* I know I've got there? I need to set out some markers."

"And you want to be sure you're getting where you want to be without climbing on other people's bodies to get there!" added Tabitha. "You need to be able to look back, in the end, and know you did your best, did the right thing. That you were true to yourself." She got up from the sofa again. "I'm going to top up your mugs and then I'm going to have to get into the Academy for rehearsals."

"And I have to see another client today," said Melanie, stretching her arms up over her head.

"And I must thank you both for helping me unravel my thoughts," said Clare. "And of course I need to get back and keep an eye on Marigold. I don't like to leave her for more than a few hours. I'm going to have to churn this all round in my mind a lot longer before I can really make sense of it. 'Though the mills of God grind slowly ...', as you used to say, Tabitha!"

"'Yet they grind exceeding small'," laughed her friend as she finished the quote.

Clare sighed, also stretching, her long legs reaching as far as Melanie's did towards the sleeping dogs.

13

I t wasn't yet a week since Marigold had landed with her, and Clare was feeling little better about it all. The child was still very vulnerable. She went out most mornings, coming back looking brighter but exhausted.

"Should we get you to a doctor," asked Clare the morning after the visit to Tabitha, looking at her pale, thin, daughter when she quietly returned to the flat,. "Or a counsellor of some sort? I feel I'm no help at all, and I want to see you better."

"I know, Mum. You've got lots to do. I love that you have your own life, your own plans. I love that you're living the life you want. And I'm sorry to barge in on it - but you'll see I had to." She glanced away.

"You can always find a place with me," reassured her mother, putting her hand on hers, "You know that."

"I know this is a nuisance. I'm interrupting things." She paused and looked away, "Actually I *am* getting some professional help."

Clare looked up sharply. "Is that what you're up to when you go out?"

"Yeah. It's a kind of Well Woman place. You know, dealing with all sorts of women's issues. They're helping me come to terms with ... what's happened to me." She took a sidelong glance at her mother. "Tiernan leaving," she added quickly.

"That's a relief," said Clare with feeling. "I feel about as much use as a chocolate teapot."

"Oh Mum, don't feel that! Just you existing is a help in itself. You know how much I admire what you're doing. You're doing it without having someone to prop you up, to validate you. You know what you want. That's how I'd like to be. I want to be able to do what I want without feeling so caught up with someone else." She poured herself some more coffee. "I hope I've learnt my lesson. But it's so hard ..." She grabbed her mug and ran to her room.

Clare sighed as she could hear the muffled sobbing under some sad music. These well women had better be good, she thought. This is going on too long.

Her thoughts were interrupted by the phone. It was Paul.

"Hey Babe," he said brightly, "how's about another date?"

"Hey Paul, nice to hear you! But I'm going to have to take a rain check on that, I'm afraid. Family stuff ..."

"I thought family didn't impinge on you," said Paul. "Clare, the independent career superwoman. Didn't know you were in thrall to anyone else."

"Ah, well the past has a habit of catching up with even the best of us," Clare laughed uncertainly. She didn't like the sound of that person Paul was describing. Was that really her? Is that how she wanted to appear? Her thoughts, still whirling from the previous day, started to solidify.

"Well, when you've got the demons back in their cupboard, give me a ring. We have fun together, you and I."

As she put the phone down again, Clare saw her relationship with Paul in a new light. Was she being so clever, having all these men-friends and keeping them at arm's length? Or was it tawdry? Was it yet another way of distancing herself, as Peggy might have suggested, if she had known about these men? Or was it playing along with men running the show, as Melanie and Tabitha had implied. Trying to behave like men behave in relationships: was it denying her own feminine values? Having to step back because of Marigold was making her question an awful lot of things.

She looked at the closed door of Marigold's room. She'd love to help her, but she could barely reach her at the moment. The fact that she'd unbuttoned a bit more just now was an advance, she supposed. But she felt sure she was holding something back. And Clare could not but blame herself for losing the connection with her daughter.

When Marigold started at Trinity, she wanted to be the self-sufficient grown-up. She wasn't, of course. But Clare reckoned that if she nagged her to report in to her Mum and went all parental and bothersome over her, it would push her daughter away. Rollo was so easy! He took everything as it came. When he needed help - money - he had no compunction in asking either Jonathan or Clare, depending on what the money was needed for. Clare was definitely the one he'd ask if he needed clothes, or a new gadget. Money for survival would come from his father. Straightforward Rollo was immersed in his impenetrably difficult studies - which Clare understood not one bit - and got on with enjoying life in a trouble-free way.

Not Marigold though! She had always been a more fanciful child with her love of old Irish legends of heroes and fairies and mysticism, fairy rings of trees and mushrooms, hills, mountains, *crannogs* - those mysterious little manmade lake islands - magic of every kind, and with a tendency to brood. As she grew older, if there were a dark side to be found, Marigold would find it. And as she was away at school, the distance between her and her mother grew. She appeared to be capable, and she was certainly heavily invested in her chosen subject. But Clare saw now just how big the distance between them had grown. Marigold's unwillingness to confide in her mother hurt her. Made her realise where she had failed her daughter.

She wondered if Jonathan had a clearer path to her mind, though she doubted it. But it was worth an ask. So she had messaged him to ring her when he was back from the yard. She could hear sad songs being played in Marigold's room. At least she'd stopped crying.

It wasn't long before the phone rang and he said, "Clare? What's up? Is Marigold alright?"

"Well, she's no worse. But not really much better. I wondered if you knew anything? Have you been in touch with her at all?"

"She hasn't spoken to me. I thought it best to let her when she's ready. It may make it all bigger than it need be if I weigh in."

"It *is* big," exclaimed Clare. "The child is in bits. She's getting some counselling, thank goodness, and it seems to be helping a little. But she's not ready to face the world again yet." She gazed out at the trees in the square below the window where she stood. "You wouldn't like to have her for a bit, would you? She loves the stables - might get her out of herself ..."

She knew it sounded lame as soon as she'd said it. She was just trying to shovel the responsibility for her daughter onto someone else. What a nasty realisation! Marigold had travelled across the Irish Sea in order to find sanctuary with her mother. And now she was trying to toss her back like a used sock.

"Er, not possible, I'm afraid. The *Arc* is in a few weeks - the *Arc de Triomphe* ... Paris," he added, as if Clare wouldn't remember. "We're busy with all the travel arrangements, getting the horses ready. Got a good chance this year, with Pacer's Lad. He's just into the age range and has done well so far this season."

"I thought as much - but thought I should ask." Clare sighed. She remembered the leggy colt that had arrived in Brownestown just before she left. "Hope Pacer does his stuff for you. I'll keep you up to speed with what happens here. Bye."

What was she thinking? She wanted to get her life back to normal, sure. But expecting Jonathan to have mysteriously become the modern man that Melanie and Tabitha had been talking about was unrealistic! And wrong. On the one hand she felt constrained and limited - no possibility of her usual carefree social life, roadblocks on her career path - and on the other hand she felt guilty. Marigold hadn't chosen to be born! It had been Clare's own choice to have her. As well as her husband's, she supposed. And she had to follow through. She thought about Peggy. There had been dark days, when she'd married Jonathan, and the rift with her father had never really healed. She had felt betrayed. The rocks who had been the basis of her life up to then had shifted and crumbled. She felt alone, outcast. But Peggy had kept the faith. She had always been there in the background, always available - once the marriage was settled and Clare was off their hands. Peggy adored her grandchildren - Rollo had been her first - and they had spent many happy holidays visiting their 'Amma'.

But Clare was not going to repeat this particular piece of history! On an impulse, she grabbed the phone again and dialled her mother's number.

"Mum." She launched without preamble. "You weren't there for me when I was in crisis. But you came good afterwards. You've always been about since then. I've been thinking about what you said. About not perpetuating this rift. I just tried to shove Marigold off to Brownestown. I feel terrible. I'm getting in a panic about work. What can I do?"

"You're a great mother, Clare. No-one could have given those two a better upbringing. You've nothing to reproach yourself with." As Peggy poured soothing words down the phone into Clare's ear, Clare started to cry.

"Oh Mam," she wept.

"It's times like these that test us. You can buckle under the weight of the burden, or you can help Marigold carry it and move to a new understanding together. I know your work's important to you. But it'll still be there in a few weeks. I'm sure you can talk to your Editor and sort something out. But where will your daughter be in a few weeks?"

"Still here, at this rate." Clare grabbed a tissue and blew her nose.

"Well, maybe she'd like to visit me. She hasn't rung me yet. I wonder why not? I'd love to talk to her. You know, Clare, life isn't made up of separate compartments." It was the same thing Tabitha had said. "You can try and make it like that, keep everything in separate boxes, but sooner or later they'll all spill over into each other. That's where the skill comes in! Running everything alongside. Isn't that something I learned while I was married to your father - servicing the genius while managing the homestead and five children with all their ups and downs?"

"I thought I'd got it all going nicely - until this happened. I've got something to offer. I know I need to focus on that. It just doesn't work when it's watered down ..." She sighed loudly. "But at least Marigold's getting some advice now, from a Well Woman place. I think it may be helping. She only told me today. She's beginning to open up a bit. Poor child is in such pain ..." she sniffed and dabbed her nose again.

"So why does she have to go to these counsellors instead of just getting counselling from you and me?" asked Peggy.

"Oh come on, Mum. You know what it's like. You don't want to tell your nearest and dearest all these private things about yourself - especially parents! Anyway, she probably wouldn't pay any attention to us, even if we said the exact same things that the counsellor said to her." Clare paused, then added, "You know, she knows what happened when I was in trouble. All those years ago with Rollo. And maybe she thinks that I'll respond the way you and Dad did."

"That was different. There were you still in your gym-slip and pregnant. Your father felt we had to make the decisions for you. Whatever it is, she's at least a little bit older."

"S'pose," said Clare dejectedly.

"You know, I'm darkly suspicious about this woman place. What is it?"

Clare said, "Well, as far as I can tell, they help women with any problems they have."

"Hmm. I thought it was just maybe to do with ... I dunno, having babies or not."

"Is that your way of saying you think it's an abortion clinic?"

"I guess so."

"Is it something you feel strongly about, Mum?" Clare had thought the same thing for a moment when she'd first been told, then remembered that this was different, as Marigold wasn't pregnant.

"You know, surprisingly, I don't. I did many years ago. But I've changed my tune. When it's looking at people, your own people, people who need some help - nah, I don't take a hard line anymore. We do what we have to do."

"That's incredibly modern of you Mum - no-one would believe you were an Irish housewife!"

"Well, we all have to change to fit into this life. And the more I see of my children and my grandchildren, the more I realise that my ideas might be really old-fashioned, outdated. So, we have to move with the times. Anyway, this woman centre. Is that why she's going there?"

"No Mum, I've told you. It's not that. They do all sorts of stuff there. Relationships, even careers I believe. And one of the things they do is counselling. She seems to be getting a lot out of it. She seems to be less frantic, and less desperate. So I'm hoping it's doing the trick."

"So how long is she going to stay with you?" asked Peggy.

"She can stay as long as she likes. No. I'll amend that. I don't want her to stay here forever. I don't, and she shouldn't. We both have our own lives to lead. I'm sure she will go back to Trinity. I'll mind her as long as she needs minding. And I hope that sooner rather than later, she'll feel the urge to go back."

"You sound a bit calmer now, my love," said Peggy. "Hope I helped a little ..."

Clare smiled, "Thanks Mum."

And so they rang off.

But wherever she turned, Clare felt stuck. Her carefully-assembled life was falling about her ears. It wasn't the logistics of working and minding her child. It was what it was stirring up in her. That was what was really affecting her. She absolutely knew what her priorities were in her life now. She knew that a great writing career was her future. Who would have thought it could all be derailed so easily? And so, she put her 'mother hat' back on the hat-stand and donned her professional 'writer's hat', and determinedly got back to work.

A while later, her equilibrium somewhat restored and more words written, she looked up to hear Marigold emerging from her room.

"Make us a coffee, would you?" Clare asked her.

"Sure," responded Marigold, a little more brightly than was usual these days. "I'm hungry too."

"Help yourself to whatever you want. I'll make dinner soon." Clare turned to watch her daughter starting the coffee. "Marigold?" she said.

"Yep?" she replied, ladling coffee grounds into the filter.

"I was talking to Mummy, Peggy - Amma. She'd love to talk to you. But she has this thing that you have to initiate the conversation. She doesn't want you to feel obliged to talk to her, and think she's prying."

"Dear Amma!" Marigold smiled as she poured cream into the mugs.

"But she still thinks of me as a little girl. I don't know if she'd understand."

"Ah, Marigold!" responded Clare with feeling. "One of the things that shows we are growing up is the realisation that people are all the same, down the ages. Same desires, same drives, same feelings." She stood up and walked over to the kitchen area. "You know all teenagers think they discovered sex? That no-one older than them understands it?"

Marigold smirked and blushed, "Yes, I do remember thinking that!" and she laughed.

"Well, everyone's gone through life. Even grandparents. And clearly they knew something about sex or you wouldn't be here! You know a bit about my story. One day I may give you more detail, but you don't need that now ... "

"There's more?" asked Marigold with a cheeky smile.

"I'm loving seeing you smiling, Pudding," Clare interjected, nudging her shoulder against Marigold's.

"Ok, I'll give her a ring. I always loved our holidays at her place. She was so indulgent - let us do anything we liked, have anything we wanted."

"That's the difference between mothers and grandmothers, in a nutshell!" said Clare, happy to remember delivering the excited children to her mother for their summer visits, all those years ago. "But of one thing you may be sure: she does love you."

As Marigold turned her big brown eyes to her, Clare added, "You are loved," and mother and daughter shared a warm hug.

14

Clare felt that at least some progress had been made. Realising she needed help with her daughter, then finding that help was in fact all around her - and being able to focus long enough to get some work done. And that was a blessing, because the next morning she was back in the office, having a planning meeting with Joanne. Since she'd scrambled to get Echo's piece in, Joanne was getting a bit more fussy about timings.

"I used to be able to set my watch by you, Clare," she said, brandishing her bright red glasses with her hand. "Don't go unreliable on me."

"Sorry Joanne, it was just a blip. Family things rose up, you know how it is."

"No." Said Joanne bluntly, back to her usual persona of the tough editor. Perhaps her kindly thoughts had been a one-off. "I keep my work separate."

"Yes, that was my strategy too," Clare smiled nervously. "But some things - well, you just have to jump in. She cursed inwardly that her carefully-erected barricades round her new life had broken down so spectacularly. Anyway, 'Echo' is now in the magazine - I love where you've placed it! And it's amazing how many pages you've given it. I know why you chose the images you did - they look fantastic. I really want to use Harriet again - she's a find!"

Mollified, always practical, Joanne moved on. "Echo's agent rang yesterday. She's tickled pink by your take on her troubled charge. She wants you to cover some of her other ailing starlets - present the case for the 'real' person behind the glitz and glamour. You interested?"

"Am I interested?!" laughed Clare, "Is the Pope a Catholic?" Out slipped the Irish expression. "I sure am. And I wanted to suggest some other pieces to you. See what you think."

Clare showed Joanne her short list of possible pieces and angles - what she'd been working on yesterday afternoon. Each name had a paragraph beside it, indicating the approach Clare planned.

Amongst them was Melanie's name, with the note, "Lots of people think animal-lovers are one-dimensional and obsessive. I'd like to show both Melanie's skill with her dogs and the warmth and humanity of the person who dedicates so much time to helping animals, and who succeeds in changing the lives of their people along the way."

Joanne slotted her glasses onto her nose, flipped through the list, and handed it back to Clare, saying, "Not mad about the Tory minister's wife, not in the present climate. And I really don't see the boyband thing working for us right now - not after their carry-on last month. But for the rest, go ahead. Give me a timetable when you've worked it out."

Clare was happy to keep the meeting short, as she was anxious to get back to check on Marigold, who'd had a major weeping session after supper the evening before, leaving both herself and her mother exhausted. Clare wondered what on earth kind of timetable would work for the new list of articles Joanne had commissioned, given the current situation with Marigold. She had no idea what to expect from one day to the next, and even less certainty over when - whether! - she could get back to her own life and pursue her own dreams again.

She whizzed through the outer office, with just a cursory "Howdy" to Nat. He turned to wave to her, always ready for a chat. Clare was so absorbed with the urgency of her new plans that she couldn't accommodate Nat's latest family story right now. She missed the look of disappointment on his face as she strode past.

After tucking Marigold up in her bed last night, she'd given Nick a ring. She'd felt in need of talking to someone without this level of intensity.

"Ah, not a great time, Clare old thing," he'd said. Clearly she'd rung at an awkward moment.

Had it taken just one cancelled date to finish this friendship off? she wondered. Friendship? Relationship? Sex-buddy? How shallow was this thing with Nick, really? And how much did she really need this kind of relationship? Yes, it was fun. But she realised she wanted things to go deeper than fun. All these churning feelings Marigold was stirring up in the three generations of her family were touching parts of Clare she had closed off for the last year or so. She definitely didn't want another full-time partner. She valued her new-found freedom far too much for that! But were Nick and Paul - and that other chap she didn't see any more ... Adrian, that was it - were they really doing her any good?

She realised the answer was in the question. If they were genuinely a good thing, she wouldn't have needed to ask it. But some adult company, someone to go places with ... that was definitely an addition to her life. Perhaps she could find different ways to do this? Something to leave till this current crisis was over, she thought. I've enough on my plate right now!

Now she was looking forward with interest to her next piece. She was going to do Melanie next. It would be different, working with someone she already knew, though she didn't know that much about Melanie's background, or what really made her tick. She knew her as Tabitha's loyal friend, someone who really cared about people - as well as seeing more in dogs than Clare had thought was possible to see.

She picked up her phone and rang her. No reply, but Clare loved Melanie's answer message, which began with a big woof before explaining that Melanie was out with the dogs and to leave a message with Heidi. Clare smiled as she left her message. As she put the phone down she reflected on what a clever idea this was - to put the caller into a good humour before they left a request.

Melanie had called her back a few hours later, and was amazed and delighted to be asked to give Clare an interview for the magazine. The kitchen windows must have been open, as Clare could hear birdsong and distant baa-ing.

"Wow Clare! Really? Thank you for thinking of me!"

"Not at all - you'll make for a very interesting piece. And we have a super photographer who'll take some outstanding photos of you and the dogs. I'm hoping for some action shots, of you doing your dancing thing with them. 'Dog Ballet' Tabitha called it. I need to see it too, to dispel my doubtless wrong ideas and find out what on earth it is. I have visions of dogs dressed in tutus. And, of course, I'd love to learn more about you - what makes you tick, you know? The person behind the dog trainer."

"No tutus, I promise!" laughed Melanie, before adding more quietly, "Oh, I'm pretty ordinary."

"You may think you are. I don't," said Clare firmly. "That's part of your charm. That you don't realise what you have."

"I hope you won't be disappointed, Clare. Perhaps you should be interviewing Dad to find out the truth." She gave her attractive light laugh. "Ooh, this sounds exciting! Photos? I wonder ..." she said, thinking out loud.

"The photographer's a free-lance," Clare guessed that Melanie was thinking about publicity for her business. "I'm sure you can work something out with her if you want to use some of the images."

So a happy Melanie opened her calendar and the two friends sorted out a date when Clare would visit. "Better fish out some clean jeans and drag a comb through my mop!" she laughed, "that's my version of dressing up. The dogs are always brushed to within an inch of their lives," she said happily. "And definitely no tutu!" she added, laughing again. Clare smiled again as she rang off, pleased to have had such a sunny impact on her friend's day.

It wasn't long before Marigold arrived home from her visit to her counsellor. She looked so tired that Clare's heart missed a beat when she saw her.

"Your counsellor is taking a lot of time with you," she said as she moved to the kitchen to prepare lunch for them both. Marigold still seemed a helpless child who needed looking after. "Are you making headway?"

"Yes," answered Marigold slowly as she sank into the armchair, her sleeves pulled down over her hands. "I'm feeling a lot better about things."

"I wish you looked better! Where's my pretty dark-haired maiden? The stuff of Irish legend and fable? I want to see you back to your full glory."

"Oh Mum!" sighed Marigold. "You see me through rose-coloured spectacles."

"Well, I'm your mother. Shouldn't I see you as the lovely creature you really are? The child I nurtured, fed, reassured, whose knees I kissed better ... and watched blossom into a beautiful young woman?"

They smiled at each other. And Clare could feel a little of the tightness sliding from her shoulders. She was letting her daughter in again. It actually felt ... strange, but satisfying.

15

Clare arrived at Melanie's place a couple of days later. She hadn't known what to expect, and she was surprised to find a humble-looking, slightly scruffy house on a large plot of land. She could see brightly-painted agility jumps and tunnels, barrels, platforms, and other paraphernalia she assumed was for dog training, in the large field behind the house. And there was a long low barn-type construction beside it.

She stepped out of her car, breathing in the fresh scents of the countryside. It was something she missed, living in the city, and always helped her to relax and enjoy life a bit more. Here there was no horsey smell as she was so used to, just lots of trees and flowers. The light but cool breeze moved the scents around in the warm sunshine, and she could hear those distant sheep again.

Melanie invited Clare into her unpretentious kitchen, like so many in the countryside sporting a powerful range cooker that belched out warmth - as evidenced by the dog beds either side of it, as close as they could be to the heat source. The beds were empty at the moment, as the one collie greeted her joyfully, while the other kept close to Melanie and watched from a safe distance.

"Hi Rhys, hello Heidi," said Clare, fussing Rhys and remembering not to stare at his shy 'sister'. "Hi Melanie - so this is where you live! It's lovely and comfy."

"Haha, that's code for scruffy and old-fashioned, I bet!" laughed Melanie. "You must visit some amazing glamorous houses in your work. I was reading the thing you did on that pop star Echo. It was touching, actually, the way you showed her."

"I like to use my pen as an artist's brush, rather than a sword!"

"I'm hoping I'll escape without too many scars ..." said Melanie anxiously, as she settled the dogs on their warm beds by the cooker and started putting coffee together.

"Don't worry, I'll spare you!" laughed Clare. "You saw the piece I did on Tabitha last year?"

"Oh yes, that was lovely. Did wonders for signups to her School - and the Junior Academy. I'm hoping this may help me too."

"Yes, it will. Definitely. Is it a hard way to earn money?" Clare placed her recorder on the table in front of her and indicated that she was switching it on. "Ok to record you?"

"Oh yes, of course – go ahead. It's a joy, actually. It's a privilege that I get to work with so many dogs. And my aim in life is to improve life for dogs - it's my contribution to the world. It's what I can do. And to do that, I need their owners to pay me! But yes, the income can be pretty irregular." Beginning to forget about the recording device, she started to flow, "I'm always having to dream up new ways to attract people, new workshops and courses. And all the courses that I need to take to increase my own knowledge add up. Fortunately I can set them against tax," she laughed. "The marketing part is the tough part, actually. Like most creative people, it's not something I do naturally."

"I get that," said Clare, jotting down a note in her notebook. "It's something that everyone who makes their passion their career comes up against. You want to be at the coalface doing the work, not having to do all the things to make that possible?"

"That's it, exactly," said Melanie as she brought over the coffee mugs, steaming invitingly despite the warmth of the room. "It's working with the dogs that gives me pleasure. The marketing is a necessary evil," she laughed. "And working with the owners is something that didn't come naturally to me at all. I had to learn 'people skills'," she grinned. "I still struggle with that by times - when somebody is being particularly unreasonable. But a few deep breaths and a count-to-ten helps to prevent the steam coming out of my ears! Hey, you won't print that?" she asked urgently, looking at the recorder, then relaxed as Clare smiled at her and shook her head.

"Don't worry, I'm not going to scare your customers away!"

"One thing I learnt early on," Melanie went on, "and I try to keep it in the front of my mind all the time - is that people won't remember what you said to them, but they'll remember how they felt about it. I want even the most spiky person to leave thinking I was a good thing. Otherwise I've failed their dog: I can't help the dog if I can't reach their owner." She picked up her mug, "I suppose that's what you do, isn't it, Clare? I don't remember all the details of your article about Echo, but I remember how I felt about her by the time I'd read it."

"You're so right! A writer has the power to change the way people look at things. There's so much manipulation in the world of writing - particularly by politicians who make their web-spinning magic an art form! I try always to use that power wisely - and kindly." She smiled, and looked back at her notebook. "And why the dog dancing? And you're going to have to explain what that means - I still have that weird image in my mind of dogs in frocks, ballroom dancing with you!"

"The name does put people off, it's true. I'll show you when we've finished in here! It's not what it sounds at all. And I love it!"

"It's a shame Harriet couldn't fix her shoot for today, but that means you can concentrate on the photos when she comes later this week. May make it easier, in fact. I'll be here too," Clare reassured her, as she saw Melanie's face looking anxious. "No stage fright, now. You're a pro, after all!"

"I love the work I do with my dogs. As you'll see, it's only Rhys I perform with - he loves showing off. I do it all with Heidi too, but that's just for our own pleasure. She's not a performer by nature, so I don't inflict shows on her."

"They are performers or not, by nature?" asked Clare with surprise, jotting a note in her book.

"Very definitely!" responded Melanie with conviction. "It's a bit like the warhorses in the Middle Ages. I read a book about it once ... the horses actually fought too! They had to be a certain type of horse to be able to learn to do that. But yes, the dogs are such individuals."

"That's true - I remember Marigold's 'schoolmaster' pony Sebastian. He was Rollo's first, till he outgrew him. Gentle, reliable - totally different character from the racehorses in the yard." She gazed at the dogs, now on their beds either side of the range. "Their feelings are important to you?"

"Their feelings are paramount!" Melanie was animated in her reply, as she threw her hands up in the air. "If my dogs are unhappy, I can't perform with them. Their happiness is so important. Nothing else matters. The two things are tied together." She took a sip of coffee and glanced down at the recorder before carrying on. "You have to balance their happiness against your own goals. If I didn't love them so much I wouldn't be able to achieve so much with them. If I tried to make them do it when they didn't want to, you'd see it in the performance. You see it a lot at competitions - dogs being made to fit in with their owner's aspirations and ambitions. Sad." She looked at the dozing dogs. "I think we need to fill the creative well with real life - love and loss. I don't think my routines would work as well as they do - be as imaginative as they are - if I didn't feel so strongly about my partners - my dogs - our shared history."

Melanie put down her mug and sat back in her chair. "I haven't told you this before, but it's important to me - to show you why I'm who I am." She paused, folded her hands in her lap and went on, "It was through the loss of my mother that my father became the marvel that he is."

"I didn't know that," said Clare. "When did your mother die?"

"Long time ago now, I was nine at the time. I'm twenty-six now."

"Ah, a bit older than my two," said Clare as she made a note.

Melanie continued, "You see, Dad had a good career in the city - he used to commute, left early every morning. But when Mum died he was bereft - of course we both were. It was awful." She leant forward again and drew her finger through a drop of coffee on the wooden table, making a pattern. "And he saw what it was doing to me, having minders all the time while he was at work, how insecure I was getting. Lost. So he chucked it. He gave up his career and stayed home. He started doing work he could do in his own time. Suddenly he was always there for me, collecting me from school, giving me my tea, helping with homework, washing my clothes - all the things Mummy had done. The house started to crumble round our ears as his income dropped, and we got used to making do. But he was there." She turned to gaze out of the window. "It was the making of me, of course. But the thing is - and he'll tell you this himself - it was the making of him too."

She went to fetch the coffee jug to refill their mugs. The dogs lifted their heads to see if there was any action, saw none, and relaxed again with big sighs. Clare gazed at Melanie, who was using the coffee activity to recover her emotions, while she thought of the enormous contrast in upbringing they had had. Melanie's father was more like Clare's mother. And there seemed to be no comparison with her own father!

"If things had stayed the same, he'd have become wrapped up in his career. Probably spent more and more time at the office. I'd have grown up behind his back. Mum - who knows - may have come to resent her lonely life with me. Eventually he'd have retired and felt trapped here, without his daily structure that would have been built up over so many years. But in fact, he became 'him'. He was no longer just a distant wage-earner for me, he was a real person - the most important thing in my life at that stage - not forgetting our pet dog at the time, of course! The warm furry presence who was always there."

Clare made another note as she picked up her mug, encouraging Melanie with her eyes and a nod, to carry on. Melanie's history was so very different from her own. Their fathers were such polar opposites.

"And this is something that made such an impact on me. That you can't look after yourself by neglecting areas of your life. And you certainly can't do your best. It's bringing the two parts together that makes it work. That's how my father achieved his calm state of fulfilment, knowing he was doing what's right. So I'm happy to be able to make my living following my passion. I never felt I had to follow the herd, work in an office, get the latest gear. It was clear to me what I was born to do. But I never forget the importance of my family in making it all possible. My family - that includes those two ragamuffins down there," she smiled, nodding at the dogs on their beds. One tail thudded in response. "If they're not well, I'm not well. If they don't like what we're doing, then we don't do it. You can't ride roughshod over other people - dogs, whatever. If they're not part of your life plans, then you may as well not bother."

She got up and leant on the back of her chair with her hands. "I'll get off my soapbox now," she laughed. "I don't often get the chance to put these thoughts into words ... you've made me think!" She tossed her red curls and said, "Want to see Rhys strutting his stuff? We'll head out to the Barn. We built it specially for training the dogs - but not just mine. Having a father who's good with his hands has plenty of advantages! I'm pretty handy with tools as well - I learnt so much from him. I use the Barn for classes too," she added as Clare picked up her things and followed her, both the dogs instantly alert and busy, trotting round them in quick circles, filling the room with activity and waving tails, and ready for whatever was coming next.

As they went out into the sunshine again and processed to the barn, Clare thought of how another father had so strongly influenced the life of another daughter. It was chalk and cheese. Melanie's father had devoted his life to his daughter and found fulfilment that way. Clare's father was dedicated to his art to the exclusion of everything else - despite all appearances. He was generous to a fault with his colleagues and students. If only he'd been as generous at home. People saw him as the great family man, spending time at home with his children, and he loved to show them off - his sons especially - when he brought them to some function. He'd snatch the smallest child from Peggy as if she were a delivery boy and parade it around triumphantly till he tired of the activity and peremptorily handed the child back. But his family knew different. He may be spending time at home, but they didn't see that much of him. They were there to serve him and enable his elevated position. She wondered how things might have turned out differently if he had been more involved with his children. She had certainly been involved with her own children, putting her creative life on hold till she could focus on it without hindrance. Only that involvement seemed to have lurched back into her life again. Melanie's talk of balance being the way to success was nagging at the back of her mind.

The Barn looked ordinary from the outside, but inside it was far from ordinary. As they opened the door it was like entering a magic cavern, with the warm scent of timber filling the air. There were full-height mirrors down most of one side, the floor was carpeted in a plain dark green, and pairs of lights hung from each cross-beam, their warm light reflected back from the many mirrors, adding a fairy-tale ballroom appearance.

"Wow!" Clare gazed around her, open-mouthed. "It's amazing! This is where you train dogs? And train their people too?" she added quickly, beginning to understand what Melanie was about.

"Yes. And I love it! The field is great for agility and nosework, but it's no good for precision footwork. It's precision that you need in Obedience competitions and, of course, dancing!"

"Why all these mirrors? Is it just to make the place look bigger?"

"Well they do have that effect, it's true. But in fact they're there to check your technique - how you look to the audience. For instance, you can't see if the dog is absolutely straight beside you without turning your head to look down, and that movement can be enough for the dog to shift his position slightly. So you want to be able to see it's right without giving lots of unwanted signals. Dogs are incredibly sensitive to our movements. That's why they're so good at this."

Clare scribbled rapidly in her book while Melanie started to unpack her bag onto a table at the front of the room, adding, "The reason sheep-dogs are so amazing is because a ewe only has to twitch an ear to indicate she's *thinking* of breaking out, and the collie shoots round to cut her off before she's even taken a step!"

"That's how sensitive they are to movement." As if to demonstrate, she asked Rhys with a small wave of her hand to jump up and lie on the table, where she selected some music, picked up a cane, then walked into the middle of the barn and called Heidi over to join her. Melanie stood, legs slightly apart, holding the cane to the ground and out to one side with her outstretched arm, and Heidi shot in from behind and sat between her legs looking up at her. Clare gasped at this simple opening move, apparently achieved without a word. Melanie pressed the remote in her pocket and the music began.

Clare was enchanted. The routine involved lots of twisting and turning from both handler and dog, Heidi winding herself round Melanie's legs then round the cane in figure-of-eight movements. The tempo changed and they processed around the barn at a fast pace, Heidi performing loops and jumps as they went, never taking her eyes off her partner - a joy to watch with her fluid movement. At one stage, Melanie appeared to be asking for a spin with an exaggerated hand-signal, but Heidi lay down flat on the floor. Clare wondered what had gone wrong. But at Heidi's response her partner feigned anger, one hand on her hip and the other waving the cane menacingly. Heidi leapt up and ran two huge circuits of the barn, as far from her as possible. Melanie did a theatrical shrug of her shoulders and tossed the cane away, at which Heidi scooped it up and ran back to her with it. They went back to some more smooth dancing, ending up with Heidi running round her backwards and slipping back into her start position between her legs exactly as the music hit its final chord.

Clare, who had been captivated as she watched the routine, burst into loud applause and laughter as Heidi jumped up into Melanie's arms, tail thrashing wildly with delight.

"That is *amazing!* I had no idea! That's an incredible display! And Heidi absolutely loves it!"

Melanie sent Heidi to hop up onto the table and join Rhys, while she walked over to Clare's chair, still breathing fast after her exertions.

"I tell you," she said, "If they didn't love it, I wouldn't do it."

"And Rhys does the same thing?"

"His routine is different - rather more demanding," said Melanie. I'm working on this one for the next round of competitions, so it's not yet finished. But I can show you a taste of it?"

"Oh, yes, please," said Clare, settling into her chair again. She'd had no idea she'd enjoy this so much.

Rhys's routine involved doing a gym workout with Melanie. He echoed every movement she made, doing the "workout" alongside her. While Melanie raised dumb-bells over her head and down again, Rhys sat upright on his haunches and waved his paws up high then down, holding the dumb-bell in his mouth. It was a delight for Clare to see him sitting in a beg beside his owner, raising and lowering his paws in time with her and the music. Melanie stood and pointed one toe forward, then the other. Rhys stood beside her and did the exact same with each of his front paws. They did press-ups facing each other, though Rhys's press-ups amusingly involved his rear end going up and down instead of the front end. Then Melanie did some yoga moves which Rhys also copied, and at one stage when she was in a downward dog position like an inverted V, Rhys crawled on his belly under her to fetch her towel from the other side, then crawled back, dropped the towel on the ground, lay on it grabbing a corner in his mouth - and rolled over, wrapping himself up in it.

"That's as far as we've got, I'm afraid." Melanie laughed as Clare burst into more applause, laughing with amazement at what this girl and her dog were able to do. Melanie stopped the music, called Heidi from the table, and both dogs trotted happily around her, tails high.

"Well Harriet is going to have a feast. The images will be stunning. Especially if she can get some close-ups of the dogs' faces. They are so wrapped up in it all."

So after getting some more business details and publicity flyers from Melanie, Clare took her leave, promising to return on Monday when Harriet would be there.

16

Clare was glad she'd had such a rewarding day, as the temporary removal of frustration helped her deal with her wan daughter when she arrived home. She was impatient to start work on this new piece, and was trying hard not to feel resentful at this cuckoo in the nest.

But Marigold still seemed to need to sleep an enormous amount, and took herself off to her room to watch a film shortly after supper, leaving Clare some time on her own.

She started work on the Melanie piece, then as she listened to her recording, she pulled up short to think about what Melanie had told her about her father. What a different life experience she'd had! Melanie's father was hands-on, always there, devoting his life to his daughter - rather as Clare's mother had been for her children, as indeed she herself had been for hers.

She thought back to her own father, when she too was at an impressionable age. Clare had always had mixed feelings about her father. He was, after all, a celebrated Irish poet, but he was often a bit distant from his children. There were seven of them in the household and Clare was the eldest. And as the eldest child is often expected to behave better than all the others put together, it could be a bit of a strain for her. She had to help her mother and keep house too. She found herself now transported back to a damp Autumn evening in Kerry, the slow, soft rain soaking everything ...

I took the mug of tea Mamaí had handed to me, ladled two heaped teaspoons of sugar into the dark brew, stirred it vigorously, and carried it carefully with both hands.

I went out of the back door, down the muddy garden path - the fresh scent of wet grass filling my nostrils, to the shed, Dad's Den. It's where my father wrote. He liked to escape from the family and the noise and doings of his many children and stay all day in his 'ivory tower' as Mam called it. Except for the days he was at the University. He spent plenty of time there, lionised by the students, according to him, and slightly envied by the other staff, as the Poet in Residence, Mícheál Ó Súilleabháin. He really was 'in residence' as he had to travel up to Dublin and spend nights there during term-time.

I had been looking forward to this visit to Dad's Den. As his oldest daughter, and one who shared his love of literature, I felt that I could talk to him. Be a bit of an equal.

I knocked quietly and went into the little room. The warmth of the gas heater knocked the autumn chill out of the cold, dark shed. As children, we always enjoyed exploring the damp corners, the spiders' webs, the tiny mouse-holes with their telltale trails of droppings.

"Here, *a Dheaidí*," I said, placing the mug on his desk, well away from his papers - I knew better than to disturb or spill tea on them! While the name I called my father sounded like the English "Daddy", I was thinking it in Irish. *Daidí* was a renowned Irish scholar, and while - like for most of the other children at school - the compulsory *Gaeilge* lessons had never been my strong point, I was happy to use it here and there, hoping he'd approve.

I waited, standing, a little away from the desk. My legs wound around each other: first my right foot squashed my left toes, then my left foot squashed my right toes, as I waited for my father to engage in conversation with me.

"Da," I said eventually, unable to hold on any longer. "*Daidí?*"

"Yes child," he responded at last, looking up from his work and noticing that the mug of tea hadn't brought itself.

"*Daidí*, you know there's this writing competition at school?" I asked.

"Ah, the writing competition," he replied with a ghost of a smile.

"Well, Declan says I ought to go in for it."

"Declan? One of the O'Donoghues?"

"Yes. We're friends. Kind of ..." I tailed off, sensing that this wasn't going well.

"If you want to win a writing competition you don't want to be messing about with this Declan article," Dad said firmly. "You want to be an artist, don't you? A creator?" he asked.

"Oh yes, *Daidí*, you know I do! There's nothing I'd like more than to be able to write like you do, and people to listen to me and like what I write. I want to write stories."

"Then you need to focus. What age have you now?"

"Twelve," I said.

"Then it's time you put that kind of nonsense out of your head and started knuckling down. You can't be creative *and* have love affairs." He was smirking, maybe at the thought of this child - me - having a love affair.

"But you have Mammy," I protested, reasonably, I thought.

"That's different," my father replied, taking a large gulp of the dark tea. "Your mother is my wife. A necessity for having a family and a home." I'd never thought of my parents as a business. Though it was true that while Mam gave us plenty of cuddles, not many were exchanged between her and Da. "That's what you'll be doing one of these fine days, I expect." He replaced the mug on the desk, taking less care of his papers than I had. "Unless you decide to devote yourself to your art. Then you won't have time for all that."

"So I can't have friends *and* write?" I asked, puzzled, in a small voice.

"Sure you can," he replied. "As long as it's just a hobby. If you want to take it seriously you need to work."

I was biting my lip anxiously. "So to be like you, I have to just ... work?"

"Yes. You have to be selfish. To protect your muse. You have to put your creativity first. If you water it down you'll get watered-down *bruscar*."

"Rubbish," I translated, to show off my Irish.

"Rubbish indeed. Not worth bothering with," he continued. "Why do you think I devote so much time to my work? I have a gift. It's my duty to honour that gift by according it its proper importance."

I stared at my father. The circle of light shed by the lamp was on his papers and on his hand that had picked up his pen again and was twirling it about in his fingers, holding it over the page as if ready to resume his work. His face was in the shadows, as was mine.

"That goes for anyone who wants to learn their craft and produce something of value. But when that someone is a female as well ... well, it's doubly difficult." He took another mouthful of tea, provided for him by his wife and his oldest daughter.

This conversation wasn't going at all as I'd thought it would. I'd expected him to be pleased that I wanted to enter the competition. I'd hoped he'd help me with it, like he used to when I was younger.

He'd always encouraged me to write. To find new words, roll them round my tongue like smooth chocolate or - as he would say - a fine wine. But the move up from National School to 'Big School' as my younger brothers called it, was out of the question since his bust-up with the Master had led to us all being schooled at home, by our mother. My father seemed to have changed his view of me. He wasn't taking me seriously.

I had hoped he'd be proud of me. Instead he seemed to see me as an interruption and a nuisance. I was shocked by what he'd said about Mamaí. I knew she spent her time looking after us and the house, and he spent his time doing ... whatever he wanted. I'd always thought they'd come together through love. But for him it seemed to be purely convenience. Mammy was dedicated to us, and to him. But he didn't seem to care deeply for her at all. How could I not have seen this before? Was it because he'd never actually said it before? Maybe because I was now twelve he thought he could give it to me straight.

"So which is it to be?" he asked, a smile curling his mouth.

"I want to be a writer, *Daidí*," I replied quietly. I felt as if I'd sealed my own fate. No more Declan. No more having fun with friends. I had to choose.

"Go on with you now," he said, bending his head over his desk. "Some of us have work to do."

I stepped out of Dad's Den and onto the wet path again, the soft rain continuing unaware, and merging with the dampness on my cheeks ...

Clare returned from this awakened memory and stared at her screen. Old sins surely have long shadows. While Melanie's father had imbued in her a sense of dedication, that any achievement was nothing if at the expense of those you loved, Clare's own father had instilled in her a feeling that if you were a creator you couldn't love. It had to be either or. She felt her face go cold at this thought. Is this where her drive came from? Had she been trying to impress her dead father all these years?

She pushed the laptop away from her as she hugged her arms round herself. She thought of Tabitha's father. A man who had been fond of his family and expressed that fondness through providing for them, doing the decent thing, working hard. And hadn't Tabitha followed that example exactly? In marrying out of a kind of duty, working so hard to try to make it work. Are we destined to follow our fathers without question? Are we inculcated with the message they give us from such an early age, and unable to escape it?

She thought of her own life. How she had always wanted to create, but thwarted by circumstance she had devoted herself to her family. Only when they were growing up and away had she felt able to develop her creative desires. And thrown herself into it, focussing on herself entirely. Why, she'd even left her family home to do it!

Was she searching for fulfilment in the wrong place? Barking up the wrong tree, as Melanie might have said? She half-smiled at her own joke. Had she headed down this lonely path and found herself in a dead end? She was pursuing a life of casual acquaintances, fleeting relationships. The only steady one was that with her distant editor. And how long would that last? On a whim Clare could be out on her ear. She had no-one really, in her work. No-one of consequence. She didn't enjoy admitting this to herself. She had chosen this way of life. And it seemed to be breaking down around her.

She sighed heavily and went over to the kitchen and poured herself a glass of wine. This required some careful thought. Could it be that Marigold was in the state she was because of Clare? This brought her up short. It shocked her. She picked up the bottle again and poured some more into her glass. She'd always loved her children, especially when they were small. She thought of thin, wiry Rollo, galloping about the garden being one of his father's racehorses, then the quieter, more introspective, Marigold, with her mop of soft dark curls, sitting beside her on the step, her toes wiggling in her summer sandals, making a daisy chain.

Charming days. Enjoyable days. She could never deny that. But she'd thought they were gone, done. And for the last year she'd parked them. She'd started them on their way then focussed on herself. Is this where things had started to unravel for her daughter?

She thought about Jonathan, her children's father. What influence had he had on their lives? He was business-like, hardworking. He got excited about his horses and their wins, and had been secretly carrying on with his trainer Aisling for years. The children had known, as she found out when she left. Or at least, Marigold had known. Rollo hadn't sussed it out, though he knew how much time Jonathan and Aisling spent together. Slower to mature than his sister, he was far more interested in pursuing his own fascination with numbers and what he could do with them.

So what had Jonathan taught them? Rollo seemed to have inherited the hardworking gene, and he enjoyed the company of his friends. But perhaps Marigold had drifted away from Jonathan's influence, seeing his duplicity, and latched on to her grandfather as inspiration. Despite Michael's early disapproval, he grew fond of his grandchildren, and would regale Marigold with stories of faeries and heroes and little people, giant hounds and leaping salmon, the stuff of the magnificent Irish legends, strong and alive to this day. She would sit cross-legged on the floor in front of him, transfixed, mouth open, eyes wide, as he became animated - perhaps assisted by the whiskey glass in his hand - as he spun his dramatic yarns, all with his own poetic twist. Rollo hadn't been interested in these stories, and would rather spend time with his father checking the horses' charts in the yard: numbers, always, in preference to words. Maybe as Marigold absorbed her Irish heritage and culture, she had taken too much of the creative work ethic from her Ampa, as Clare had done. She had told Clare how much she admired her purpose and focus. Maybe her own dedication to her work had prevented her expressing herself freely to Tiernan, and now it was too late. Maybe she was in danger of going down the same track as Clare - single-mindedly.

Clare had been talking to her mother one time, who had said, "Your father wasn't the hero you seem to think he was."

And into Clare's mind had slid another image back from the mists of many years ago. It was in Brownestown. Michael had been visiting them and they were all sitting round the table after their meal, Marigold perched in her high chair beside Clare. Rollo was about four. His speech wasn't great at that time - he'd been a bit of a slow starter with words.

But Rollo leaned across the table where he sat on his father's lap and with a shy smile offered Michael one of the prized dinosaurs from his toy box. Michael took it, put it in his pocket, and carried on talking about himself.

Rollo's face fell. He reached towards his grandfather wanting to get his dinosaur back. Michael by turns teased him with the toy and ignored him.

"Give it back to him," said Clare. "Give him back his dinosaur." Michael ignored her, ignored the child, carried on talking. Rollo scrambled down off Jonathan's lap and ran from the room, trying not to let his tears be seen. Clare had shot her father a glance, snatched the dinosaur from his pocket and hurried upstairs to find Rollo in his bedroom. He was sobbing on his bed, completely bewildered by his Ampa's behaviour. Clare picked him up and held him and calmed him, encouraging him to show her what his dinosaurs got up to when she wasn't there. The big dinosaur was rather more aggressive than usual as it pounced on the littler ones.

This was another of those events she had blocked from her mind. She'd been picking and choosing what to remember. And she had been remembering the public side of her father's life - his literary awards, his acclaimed book releases, his poetry readings - conveniently ignoring the failures in his private life. After all, Peggy had left him and taken all the children with her. And none of his children had spent much time with him in his later years, choosing to distance themselves. Had that been a price he felt worth paying? But that was as mad as what she was doing now with her own life! Dividing it up into sections. Not letting one side of her influence the other. Unreal. Deluded. Mad.

She drained her glass and set it back on the table. Making her own bed and lying on it was one thing. Making it for her children, quite another. Peggy had talked about not passing problems down through generations. How much we influenced our offspring! Even when we thought we were encouraging them to be themselves. The example of how we lived spoke so much louder than the words we'd tell them. Clare had always been devoted to the children as they grew up. But now? She had pushed the boat out and expected them to fend for themselves while she ... followed exactly in her father's footsteps of self-aggrandisement and isolation. She had taken on board everything he'd taught her - without realising it! - and it seems she had never stopped trying to be accepted by him, to impress him, even though he was now gone.

Had Marigold got caught up in this "creativity versus love" idea? Had she in fact pushed Tiernan away till he decided to leave?

It was only the other night when she had said, "I think my work is so important that I need to devote myself to it more."

"What about your friends? What about larking about through your time at university? Isn't that partly what it's for?"

"I've done enough larking." She toyed with the fringe on her skirt. "I've got some good friends there, but it's time for me to knuckle down again. No more nonsense!" She smiled bravely at her mother, her face working to prevent more tears.

Clare shuddered to think that it may be all her fault that Marigold was now so desolate. Hers and her father's. His thoughts reaching like tentacles down through her to her beautiful, once-sunny, daughter.

She realised that Marigold's crisis was giving her a lot to think about, causing her to re-evaluate her own life. Was she at a dead end? Or was she still on the right path? A sinking feeling started in her stomach and spread all over her body, making her feel sick and weak. If her body was telling her that something was wrong, then something must be very wrong. All this rationalising the situation was no use if it made her feel sick! It was a pretty strong indication that she was not in alignment with what she really believed. She was saying one thing and doing another. Making herself out the sensitive and perceptive writer, while ignoring her own true relationships entirely. Thinking that her life fulfilment could come from denying her heart. Some serious thinking and adjustment had to be done. She sighed noisily, shut her laptop, and went to start the dinner.

17

Marigold had gone off to her well woman place. There was a drop-in cafe there, she had explained, so she could talk to people. Clare insisted she eat at least something before going out.

"Ok Mum," she said, like a bored teenager, nibbling a grape and not resisting when Clare slotted a bar into her pocket. Clare wondered when she'd stop all this navel-gazing and snap out of it. She was beginning to resent Marigold's neediness. For all her thoughts of the previous day, when it came down to it she was impatient. She hated seeing her own irritation. But she'd never been the earth-mother type, not deep down. Or so she had always thought.

But truth be told, it was her own confusion she was resenting! She had thought she had it all just as she wanted it. And now all these thoughts were creeping into her head - that she'd been on the wrong track all along.

This was devastating. It undermined everything she'd believed. The revelation that she had been trying to impress her father all these years, to live up to his impossible ideal, had shaken her. She'd really thought she was her own person. That she took decisions that were right for her.

Now she felt a puppet. And her father, as she was now admitting to herself, had feet of clay.

Rollo appeared on her phone with a bleep. Bless him, he really cared for Marigold, but he was happy to keep the problem at arm's length. Who could blame him? His sister was not his responsibility - he had his own life to lead. But Clare was happy to see his cheerful face with his floppy dark hair over his forehead.

"You look quite the scientist these days," she laughed, after she'd given him the latest on Marigold, which wasn't very much.

"Have to look the part, Mum," he rejoined. "I'm giving lectures to the First Years now, so I need to impress them," he laughed back.

"Wow, so now you're teaching too?"

"Yep. My tutor put me forward for it. It's a bit of an honour, actually ..." He shuffled shyly in his seat and glanced away.

"I bet it is! I can see you making a career in Academia. Would suit you. I'm proud of you - not least because I struggle to add two and two."

"Well, if you ever want a sum added up, you know where to come! Two plus two is straightforward enough. It's when one plus one equals three that you have to worry." He gave an enigmatic smile. "Bye Mum."

Clare watched the screen go blank and puzzled over his parting shot. Whatever did he mean? But before she had time to try to work it out, her phone rang again straight away and it was Peggy.

"Marigold has rung me," she began. "She's very mixed up, poor girl."

"I know, Mum. She doesn't seem to be getting much better."

"I think we only know the half of it. She's keeping something to herself. There's more to this than she's letting on, you mark my words."

"Well, I wish she'd get it off her chest and let me get back to work. It's really hard trying to write with all this going on. As soon as I start something it seems I'm interrupted. I hate looming deadlines! Family conflabs all the time, soul-searching, I dunno," she ended lamely.

"Have you talked to her?"

"I try. But she's not very forthcoming. I'm hoping that if I give her space she'll feel better about opening up. You know that big piece I did about Echo, when I visited you?"

"Mm-hm."

"They want me to do more of those. But I can't get started. There's too much turmoil. It's very frustrating. I thought I had everything worked out, Mum."

There was a pause before Peggy answered. "We never have everything worked out. We're always learning. And we're always in a new place. Every moment is new. So as soon as we get things right, they're wrong again."

"That sounds a bit Irish to me!" Clare gave a short laugh. "Like the fellow who, when asked for directions, answered very slowly, 'If I were going there, I wouldn't start from here'!"

Peggy's voice smiled as she said, "It may sound backwards, but it's true. We're continually in motion, continually adjusting, changing. You remember what we were talking about the other day? How wrong I had been to follow your father blindly over your situation back then. You do know I've been trying to make it up ever since?" She paused and Clare could hear her adjusting the phone to her other ear. "I'd like to help more now. I wonder if Marigold would like to stay with me for a bit so you can get your work issues sorted?"

"That's really kind of you, Mummy." Clare's use of the childish diminutive was a clear indicator of her feelings of helplessness right now, of dependence.

"I'll suggest it to her," said Peggy. "I'll get back to you later. Bye. Oh, and we're all in this together. You're not alone." And she rang off.

Yet another strange parting comment. Was this a veiled criticism of Clare's distance from the family over the past year? She felt all too ready to jump to conclusions that people were getting at her. Clare felt besieged, and it made her defensive. She was still in turmoil from her thoughts of last night. A disturbed night with little sleep hadn't helped. How did these things happen? How did she find herself in this impasse?

She had always hated the thought of being controlled, of having to do someone else's bidding, her own desires squashed. She'd had to do exactly that when she married Jonathan. She was trapped, felt she had no choice but to put her 'real' life on hold – no triumphant university career for her.

She smiled at this melodramatic turn of thought. Truth be told, she'd had a great life in Brownestown. Many women would have killed for that easy existence - big house, nice cars, entertaining, staff, no money worries. But it hadn't been the life she'd planned for herself. Her burning desire she had put aside. Why? Why on earth had she shut off a huge part of her life in this way?

She could easily have made time in her day to write! She'd been single-minded about being the best mother possible, and being seen to be, as well. It was a point of pride with her that her children were always beautifully turned out, beautifully behaved. She'd felt then that she couldn't dilute her art by mixing it with rearing a family, being the wife of an important man. And she'd looked ahead to the time when she'd be able to take up the life she'd lost, live true to her creativity. She'd marked time for years so that she could find perfection. She'd felt that it was absolutely the right thing to do. The only way. How crazy this was, looked at now in the cold light of day!

These were her father's words and beliefs, not hers: the result of his heavy influence on the way she thought. This rigid idea was simply his way of being in the world. It was not the truth, the unbendable truth - fact. It was a mantle she had taken on.

Clare had always thought of those women who wrote while raising a family as somehow second-class. Not serious. Though she was working as a journalist right now, she wanted to do more serious writing - a novel for sure - as well as more in-depth features, making an impact on the world. But she had used her father's words as an excuse for dodging the work. This made her stomach lurch. She knew she was being ridiculous about those who managed work and family. Of course it was possible! And of course it didn't mean they were producing poor-quality work. Think of all the people who had produced masterly work - writing, painting, composing - in the most difficult and oppressive circumstances!

And she had allowed this perfectionist ideal to push her desires away. It was easier to do nothing than to attempt to combine her plans with her actual life. Thanks, Perfectionism! What a shock to realise that rather than do something less than perfectly, she'd opted to do nothing at all.

Suddenly everything she'd thought was true was being challenged. What she'd based her life on was shifting. She had believed implicitly what her father had told her, and stuck to it like glue. It had seeped into her being and sat there within her as a fact. She had accepted it without question. Hadn't her mother just told her how she'd changed her views? And Peggy had changed her life entirely to escape her husband's influence, by decamping with five young children - even moving country - so they could go to school again.

Clare had never thought of it like that. She saw now what a great sacrifice her mother had made in order to retain her own integrity. And yet when Clare had become pregnant, Peggy had been quick to agree with Michael and toe his party line. There were tentacles ... that could reach out and pull you back to old thought patterns.

And this is where she felt she'd been stuck. For years. It had taken her daughter's crisis to rock her new boat sufficiently to make her question everything.

What she thought was truth was not. It was what she'd always accepted as how the world is. But it's not. As Peggy had said just now, every day gives you the chance to re-create yourself. Wasn't Echo demonstrating exactly that by how she was handling her present adversity! And Tabitha had done just that. She'd re-created her life almost entirely so that she could follow her passion. And what about Melanie, who pursued her love of working with her animals by teaching others, in order to fund her own journey of discovery.

This was an opportunity for her now to re-create her life. And so, what belief would she base it on? Perhaps that she could do everything! That she could let her work and her family, her friends, all mix together. That she didn't have to isolate one thing from the next?

Like everyone, Clare craved love. But she'd been wearing a suit of armour for the last few years, to insulate herself from it. She could enjoy shallow friendships with the men dancing round the edge of her life, and she was happy to spend time with her girlfriends. The deep ties to her own family she was resisting. Keeping them in their separate boxes. Wanting to cut them off, cut off that part of her heart that felt so vulnerable.

She thought she was protecting her soul by keeping her family at a cool distance. Was she afraid that letting them in would somehow pollute her great art? She snorted with derision at her own arrogance.

By now, Clare had got up from her table and was striding anxiously back and forth round the room. The agitation in her mind needed physical expression. She grabbed her coat, phone and keys and set off on a walk round the streets near her home. She would find a park and think there. Being in nature, in the fresh air, always helped clear her head. And walking would tire her physical agitation.

After half an hour or so, she found a park. A little oasis in the busy city: it did not have the wild vistas of County Kerry - the Kingdom - she'd grown up with, or the neater, tended views of County Meath where she'd reared her own children. But it was a touch of nature. She chose a bench under some trees, sat with a sigh and took out her phone. She'd talk to Tabitha. Tabitha was so sensible - she was always a steadying influence. And heaven knows, she had been through so much herself and emerged triumphant and unsullied. She was a quiet person, humble, but she knew a thing or two about life.

"Ah, you're lucky to catch me," said Tabitha, answering the phone. "I'm just off to the Academy."

"You usually start later, don't you?"

"Well, one of Gerard's children is ill. Seems it's meningitis."

"Oh Lord," said Clare, "that sounds bad."

"They hope they've caught it early enough. Gerard's wife knew straight away that something was very wrong, and insisted on getting the doctor out straight away. Mothers really know their children!" she laughed ruefully, as Clare felt a stab in her heart. "Anyhow, Gerard has been camped out at the hospital for the last two days, so I've been covering his classes."

"That's kind of you!"

"What's it all about, if you can't help a friend in dire need? I can tell you, if Esme or Cariad were that ill, I'd be with them - never mind any work commitments!" she laughed. "But you know - putting his child's predicament out of my mind while I work - I'm really enjoying it! His students are mostly the usual age, eighteen plus, which is much older than I'm used to, so that's different for me for a start, and he also has some private mature students. Now *they're* really interesting! I have to use a completely different approach with them. They have such fixed ideas."

"Really?" asked Clare, thinking of what she'd just been ruminating on.

"Yes. They have ideas about what's right and wrong. What they can or can't do. What they're good at, and what they think they could never achieve. I suppose we all have these beliefs we've picked up somewhere in our lives. I see it as my task to break those down, show them a new way."

"I seem to remember you were labouring under some inappropriate beliefs yourself only a year ago?"

"You're absolutely right, Clare! And I'm eternally grateful to you for helping me see how wrong I was. Here, I've got to fly - can't be late. Did you want something in particular?"

"Just talking to you is a tonic, my friend," said Clare, wholeheartedly. "And I think you've answered my question! Talk soon, bye."

And so Clare felt things beginning, just beginning, to fall into place. She stretched her arms up in the air, got up, and strode purposefully back to her flat to focus on the Melanie piece - the piece that had catapulted her into all this thinking!

18

The phone rang sharply into Clare's thoughts on Monday morning. It was only 8 o'clock! Way too early to deal with calls. Who on earth was ringing her at this hour? A quick look at the caller ID showed her it was Melanie. Perhaps she was panicking about today's photoshoot. She sat up in bed, swept her hair out of her eyes, cleared her throat, and answered.

"I'm really, really sorry," Melanie started, breathlessly, "but I have to cancel the photos today. Can you tell Harriet? I don't have any way to reach her. I do hope she hasn't set out already ..." Her voice was full of anxiety.

"Hey, what's happened? You don't want to do it?"

"Oh no, it's not that! I've been looking forward to it - I've been getting some more practice in on the things I think would make good images. No - Rhys has damaged his cruciate - that's a ligament in the back leg. It's absolutely essential that he gets total rest. Cruciates are a pain - if they don't heal properly they can interfere with movement for ever: it could destroy his career," she added, in obvious distress.

"Oh no, that's dreadful," Clare felt that awful things were happening to all her friends at once, what with Tabitha having to help out in Gerard's drama.

"But you know, even if he could never perform again, I'd still feel the same. These dogs are the most important things in my life - plus my Dad of course! Nothing else matters. Anyway, it'll be at least a week before he can start using his leg again. For now he's shut in his crate looking fed up."

"I suppose you can't settle him down with a good book ..." said Clare.

"I wish!" laughed Melanie. Clare was glad to hear her laugh. "It seems cruel, keeping him locked up. But you know how lively he is - he could so easily make it very much worse with just one jump or wiggle. And it makes me feel wretched too, to see him there while I take Heidi out. Look," she said, suddenly getting back to her anxious voice, "I know this is wrecking your schedule. You know they say you should never work with children or animals! It's something Tabitha jokes about, that being her daily life. If it means the whole project has to be scrapped then I quite understand. I'm so sorry for putting you through all this work for nothing ..."

"No no, don't worry," soothed Clare, cursing inwardly. "I can delay the piece. I'm very pleased with it actually - should do wonders for your business too. But I'll tell Harriet, don't worry about that. I'll do it straight away when we get off the phone. And keep in touch with me on how Rhys is. Give him a kiss on the nose from me." She realised with surprise that she was actually quite fond of all these dogs who were now in her life. "And as soon as you're ready we can re-schedule. Does that work?"

"Oh, thank you, Clare. It's all so awful ... I'll let you know - bye now. And sorry ..."

Clare sighed as she put the phone down. That was her day gone up in smoke. And her next article. Now she was going to have to approach the slightly thorny Joanne with yet another scheduling problem.

Clare had been working hard on Melanie's piece, and was impressed with what she'd written. No-one could fail to empathise with this girl and her life - whether they were interested in dogs or not - but they'd also be impressed with her ability, her confidence and commitment, and her genuine love for her animals. Such clarity of vision in one so comparatively young was uncommon. They'd see that there was a lot more to her than simply an animal-mad girl playing about with dogs all day. We all have hidden depths, and one of Clare's aims in the article was to awaken the reader to looking inside to find their own. And it should certainly boost enquiries for Melanie's dog training services. Money was clearly not a driver for Melanie, rather the joy of showing people how to relate to their animals (and each other!) in a better, more mutually beneficial way. But judging by her slightly dilapidated house and her much-loved but battered van, she could certainly use a bit more income.

She had been looking forward keenly to today's photoshoot, and the chance to see some more of Melanie's magic. She could see why Tabitha had been so blown away by her gentle approach - making her dog an equal partner instead of ordering it about - and she could see how it was reflected in Tabitha's relationship with her own two dogs, her child-students, and indeed everyone fortunate enough to cross her path.

She got up and dressed, watching the clock for when she'd be able to ring Zenith. When she did, she was relieved to find that Harriet's appointments person would be able to catch her straight away and stop her leaving for the job.

The crisis temporarily dealt with, she smiled as she made her coffee, remembering something similar to Rhys's plight years ago. Jonathan had thoughtlessly taken Rollo out with him on the gallops for hours. This would have been fine a few years later on, but Rollo was only five at the time, and walking for miles in his wellie boots left him with a badly-swollen foot, and pain when he tried to walk. After consultation with the doctor, who had prescribed painkillers, ice, and rest, she had said to Rollo, "You have to lie down on the sofa in the living room and watch television for the rest of the week. No school. I'll bring you anything you need. You have to stay with your foot up and *not move*." This last for her fidgety, never-still, little boy.

He had gaped at her, his jaw falling, "I have to watch *teilifís* for a week?" he had asked with disbelief, television normally being strictly rationed as Clare would rather they played outside than collapsed zombie-like on the sofa in front of the tv.

"That's it, son - a dream come true for you!" So they'd spent a week with wall-to-wall Sesame Street and Thomas the Tank Engine. Having a tall aerial on the highest point of their tall house meant that they could pirate the English television channels from the North of Ireland, as well as get the Irish *Raidió Teilifís Éireann* service. After a few days she wondered if she'd ever be able to bear to hear Ringo Starr's voice again. Marigold had enjoyed her brother's confinement and moved her entire family of dolls into the living room, where Rollo had to have them arranged around him and have various parts of his body bandaged by her 'nurses' - a collection of bears, a clown, and a lamb. Clare wouldn't let Marigold touch his bad foot, but at times the long-suffering Rollo looked like a mummy from her ministrations, horse bandages being easily found in their house.

Good things could come out of any situation, she thought, as she shook the memory of her sweet little children out of her mind and came back to the present. Melanie's dog problem really wasn't her fault. She'd just have to explain to Joanne that she was going to start on the next project and put Melanie on hold.

Marigold was still in bed. With a sudden shaft of light, Clare thought that today having become empty would be a marvellous opportunity to connect with that little girl again. It would get Clare out of herself, and hopefully do the same for Marigold.

She was beginning to feel things slipping and sliding - cracking and howling - as new ideas were being born. Now she'd found the source of what had governed her life thus far, she was going to fashion her own life from her own ideas in future, not follow a pre-destined path set by others.

She was beginning to luxuriate in this new plan. And with each passing day it became more natural, more obvious, more welcome. Clare checked over her article calendar, preparing to talk to Joanne to explain the postponement of 'Melanie' and outline her revised schedule. Then she started to get breakfast ready, to see if she could tempt Marigold to eat before they set out.

19

The very first thing she had to do was talk to Joanne. Clare knew the time of her daily editorial meeting, so waited till that was likely to be over before ringing her. The meeting must have gone well, as Joanne was in a welcoming, sunny mood. She was a great editor, and Clare supposed that her turbulent mood swings were part of her success in some way. But it could make approaching her quite difficult at times.

So the disaster scenario Clare had been picturing in her mind didn't quite come to pass, although Joanne was far from happy about her request to postpone the dog piece - as she called it, and mess up her schedules. At first she wanted Clare to come in to the office straight away to discuss it.

Clare bridled. This was a moment to test out her new resolve. Would she meekly do as she was bidden or would she actually hold to her plan to go out with Marigold for the day? She grasped the nettle and said, "Listen, you don't need me to take up any more of your time - you ok'd the list of people you wanted me to start on next. What say I take the first two and get going with those? I can ring them straight away, and fill the gap left by this postponement."

Seeing the problem dissolving with Clare's willingness to re-arrange,

Joanne returned from her prickliness to her earlier good humour. They picked out a couple of candidates together. Just as they were ringing off, Joanne said, "By the way, Echo's agent is now talking about a follow-up piece on her, for one of our other titles. Suitable for syndicating to the local magazines. Her stock has soared again since your piece. You did a great job at halting the slide in her popularity. People are seeing her differently, and she's had a few of those daytime tv couch interviews. You can start work on that too, though it won't be needed for a couple of weeks."

Clare was thrilled! Not only were things moving, but she'd actually made a stance and held to her new plans for her life. Was this what work-life balance was all about, she laughed! Maybe it's not so bad ... She felt a weight slipping from her shoulders as she realised she could manage Joanne without fear of getting the sack.

By the time Marigold dragged herself from her bed to the bathroom and emerged into the day, Clare was happily booking appointments for her new schedule. She was on the phone talking to Harriet when Marigold came into the room, so she gave her a big smile and gestured her to the kitchen where she'd made fresh coffee and set out some croissants and raspberries.

"Yes, such a shame about today, Harriet. But you'll enjoy it when it happens. I was astounded at what she can do with ... just a dog."

"Don't let Nat hear you say that," laughed Harriet. "You know his house is a jumble of dogs and kids? He loves them."

Clare laughed. "I quite like my friends' dogs actually. They're individuals, and really well-behaved - don't jump all over me or slobber. We always had dogs, of course, on the estate, but they were working dogs, part of the scenery. They all looked much the same to me, always in a heap round the Aga. I never bothered enough to find out about them, their characters. It's a late flowering for me! Anyhow, I'll confirm those dates with you as soon as I get them. I love what you can do with your camera - you see right into people. Don't think you'd better take any pictures of me!"

Marigold joined her at the table, as Clare made her goodbyes, put down the phone, closed her laptop, sat back and smiled at her.

"You look a bit brighter today, sweetheart," she said, picking up her mug too.

"I think things are beginning to change," said Marigold mysteriously. "I'm feeling a bit more comfortable. I've started to work again."

"That's good! So are you feeling ready to think about going back to Trinity?"

"Not yet. But I'm seeing light ..." she smiled wistfully.

"Look. My plans have changed for today. Something got cancelled so I'm free. Let's go out! We can go to the shops if you like, or just wander about and stop at a cafe. What do you think?"

"I'd like that, Mum!" Marigold looked up appreciatively. "It's wonderful you've got a day off. You work so hard. I admire your dedication - you're so single-minded. But it would be nice to just spend some time together: yes!"

Clare winced inwardly. Her daughter had been with her now for nearly two weeks. She'd fled to her for sanctuary when she'd hit rock-bottom. And how much undivided time had she actually given her? She really had to do better. Well, she'd made a start already by keeping today free. She did love this girl. And that love had to encompass everything about her - 'warts and all' as Oliver Cromwell had famously instructed Peter Lely when commissioning his portrait.

It really was time she put someone else first in her life again, as she had done for all those years up till recently.

So they set off on their outing, visiting clothes shops, bookshops, a woo-woo shop full of unicorns and rainbows and strange scents - all sorts of shops. Marigold picked out a couple of books she'd wanted, and Clare bought her a warm brightly-coloured jumper ("Mum! Look at this!" she'd said as soon as she'd spotted it) as well as a new pair of boots for the coming winter. By the time they reached a cafe they were both done with shopping and crowds.

As they were stepping into the cafe - Marigold going straight to the Ladies - who should be leaving, but Paul.

"Hey Clare," he beamed, "great to see you! I enjoyed the other evening - when are we going to schedule a return match?" he smiled knowingly.

Clare looked anxiously towards her daughter, who glanced over her shoulder while pushing open the door.

"Ah, Paul - lovely to see you too." Clare felt uncomfortable. Her new thoughts didn't sit right with this relationship with Paul. She'd given him little thought since the day Marigold crashed back into her life. She enjoyed his friendship and their banter - but she realised she just didn't want any more at the moment. "Yes, it *was* fun. But right now is not a good time. Still got a lot on my plate - family stuff," she added. "I'll ring you - gotta rush now. Bye!" and she turned and walked fast to the counter to join the queue, catch Marigold, and place their orders.

Regretting how short she'd been with him, she turned and gave a quick smile and wave as he looked after her with puzzlement. She put an arm through Marigold's as she joined her, to demonstrate to him what she had to focus on. And she felt a surge of freedom wash through her. She puzzled over this for a moment before focussing on enjoying choosing coffee and cake with her daughter.

"Nice-looking bloke," said Marigold, as she selected a slice of lemon meringue pie. She turned to her mother with a raised eyebrow.

"Just a friend through work," said Clare, and wondered if she could hear a cock crowing in the distance ...

As they sat down with their drinks and food, the noise and clatter of the cafe subsiding a little as they chose a corner table, Marigold said, "I know I've been a pain. I've interrupted your work - your life. I've got you a little something as a thank you." She handed a small packet to Clare, who was surprised that Marigold had thought of this at such an absorbingly difficult time for her. She opened it carefully, finding a tiny amethyst on a silver chain.

"Oh, Marigold," she exclaimed, holding it up under her chin with both hands, "I love it! Thank you! Here, do it up for me, will you?" Clare wanted Marigold to get behind her so she wouldn't see the tears in her eyes.

Marigold got up and fastened the necklace, then placed her hands on her mother's shoulders, saying, "There - done!" Clare turned towards her, picking up her hand and kissing it.

"You're very special to me Marigold. I don't deserve you."

Marigold laughed and touched her mother's shoulder again before returning to her seat. "You deserve better than me, Mum."

"Oh no, none of that! You are you. You're already as special as you can be, and I love you dearly. I know I don't say that often enough. It's been a difficult few weeks ... but I wouldn't have changed it for the world." As she said the words she recognised the truth in them. The truth she'd been pushing away with the hustle and bustle of what she had thought was more important. So had she been living a lie? Was she wasting her energy pursuing this career if it could so easily be displaced by a random daughter bursting in on her?

"There was a lovely silver fairy," said Marigold as she smiled warmly at Clare, determined to bring the conversation back to safer ground. "That's what caught my eye in the shop. But I thought that was definitely too woo-woo for you."

"Of course, you're into all this mystical stuff, aren't you."

"It's not as mad as you think, Mum," said Marigold as she actually tucked in to her pie. "We were up at Tara - you know, the Hill of Tara?"

"Yes - you could see it clearly from the kitchen in Brownestown. I used to love looking out at it and thinking of all the people who had visited there over the centuries. An important holy place, isn't it?"

"That's it. A place of continuous worship for five thousand years - that's quite something. Think of all the different religions there were in that time! But it seems to have an aura that attracts all this - it's a spiritual place. Well, we were up there with divining rods, seeing if we could find some ley lines," she took a sip of coffee.

"And ...?"

"The rods went mad! They were spinning round like windmills! There are ley lines everywhere there, criss-crossing. It's when you see something like that that you realise that all this woo-woo stuff is ... not so way out."

Clare was excited and relieved to see Marigold so animated - this was the most like herself she'd been since she'd arrived! She determined to keep the conversation going on this tack.

"I didn't know you used divining rods. I remember a man coming to locate a troublesome old drain pipe at Brownestown. He walked up and down holding his rods out in front of him. I thought he was bats - but he found the pipe right out in the paddock in no time at all. Then he located exactly where it was cracked and leaking. Amazing. It saved hours of work. They'd have had to dig the whole length before they found it if this old guy hadn't used his bits of bent bull-wire!" She drank some more of her coffee, enjoying the scent as she held the mug under her nose. "So I do believe in some of this stuff!"

"Well, I believe in lots of it," said Marigold with a smile. "And when you can actually see it working - like you did, it shows that there's an awful lot we just don't comprehend. A friend of mine used a pendulum over a map to locate a well which wasn't marked there. When we reached the field we found the pendulum was exactly accurate! Now how on earth does that work? We don't know - we just know that it does."

"Well that's very true, I'll give you that. Sometimes we just have to accept mysteries. So much of life is baffling!"

Clare felt her amethyst again. She was touched by her daughter's gesture - heaven knows, Marigold had little enough money on her grant - and Clare kept touching the necklace as they ate.

"You'll have to tell me where this shop is. Now I know what you'd like for your birthday!" Clare smiled and munched her cake thoughtfully, then said, "You love looking after people, don't you."

"It's nice to see people happy. And yes, I'd love that fairy pendant!"

"Done. We can go and get it on the way back. There's an advantage to me earning decent money!" she added. Then Clare reflected, gazing into the middle distance, "I've always been pretty self-centred myself."

"No! You were always a great mother to us!" protested Marigold, leaning forward earnestly. "You were the obvious choice for me when I .. when I needed a break. Why on earth would you say that?"

"I've always been a perfectionist, wanting to do things to the best of my ability," thought Clare aloud, gazing into the distance in her mind. "So when circumstances dictated Motherhood, that's what I did. But I always felt I should be producing something - other than children and meals," she smiled, looking at Marigold to see how this landed. If she was learning something ground-breaking about herself, she had to pass it on.

"I felt I was marking time till I could express myself through what I could create."

"You created me. And you formed me, nurtured me, helped me become who I am. Maybe I'm not a good advertisement for all that work!" she grinned. Clare snorted and waved her hand as if to brush away such a nonsensical statement from Marigold as she went on, "But isn't it all part of who you are? And who you are governs what you do. I do read your articles, you know."

Clare looked up at her in surprise. "You do?"

"I do!" she laughed. "I have to creep to the newsagents with a paper bag over my head so my classmates don't see my magazine choice!" They both laughed at this nod to intellectual snobbery. "But you know the way you're able to portray people, show their innermost thoughts without being a nasty intrusive hack? Well, that comes from you being you. And you being you is the result of your life up to now. All of it."

"How come you're so perspicacious at such a tender age, when I'm only just beginning to see this?"

Marigold smiled and continued, "But devoting yourself to your art as you do - that's something to be proud of. It's something I aspire to. I'd love to just drop everything and do my thing, as you have! You're a great role-model for me, Mum. But I'm so glad you steered me towards University. I've found it's been amazing to allow me to really focus on what's important to me."

"And that included Tiernan?" asked Clare tentatively.

"I thought it did. But I see my mistake now. My work is important. That will always be there. But Tiernan's shown that he's not always there. It's easy to make a choice."

"You're sounding a lot older than your years, and that's a bit of a worry. You're young! You should be propping up the student bar, painting the town, doing crazy things, enjoying life - all of it."

"There's plenty of time later - if I want to."

Clare made a mental note to revisit this seriously wrong idea. Time flew by, as well she knew! Marigold would never get this opportunity again to let her hair down, with no commitments. But she didn't want to interrupt the flow - it was wonderful to hear her daughter opening up like this, so much more like her old self than she'd been for weeks.

"For now," Marigold hurried on, unaware of the effect of her remark, "I'm firmly focussed on my studies, what I can do to promote Irish studies - not only in Ireland, but all over the world. I believe that what forms a nation is important to understand, not just for those people, but for anyone interested in the human condition."

"This kind of thinking is one of the things I missed through not going to University at your age. I can imagine you all, having intense discussions long into the night to put the world to rights. At the Open University summer camps we were all older. Our opinions more formed already. We mainly discussed literature. Interesting." Clare thoughtfully picked up the last crumbs of her cake and licked her fingers.

It was only later she realised that her daughter was thinking the exact same thing she had been thinking. That you can't have love and create. It hit her deep in her stomach. Was this what she was perpetuating down the generations, as Peggy had said, referring to how she had failed to respond to Clare's needs so long ago now? She knew absolutely, that now was not the time to start shaking Marigold's beliefs. She was still very vulnerable, and she needed to steady the ship, not rock it. How much did a father influence a daughter, and then a mother influence her child? How much do we accept and believe without question, as these ideas go down from generation to generation?

20

Next day dawned bright and clear - one of those crisp October mornings when you needed to be out in the countryside, inhaling the fresh cold scents of crunchy leaves underfoot and the smoke of distant bonfires. But that's not where Clare was. She was grappling with work and family problems in her city flat.

Marigold went off to her drop-in place again while Clare started getting her work organised. She had the nasty sensation of things slipping out of her grasp. Her usually tightly-managed schedule, her appearance of being totally in control, was crumbling. It was unnerving. In the year she'd been working with Joanne she'd never let her down. Now it seemed to be happening all the time. One minute she was devoted to her work and keeping everything in line, and then she tossed it all to the winds by taking a day off! She had enjoyed the day - more than she had anticipated, and much more than she wanted to allow - and yet it had thrown everything asunder, and she was fighting to catch up.

Was she trying to fit a quart into a pint-pot, as her grandmother had so colourfully put it? She needed to organise this new life of hers - for it felt that Marigold would be around and needy for a good while longer - and get things working again. She was suddenly getting noticed, getting enquiries, getting busier, fielding approaches from other editors. It was all very gratifying - and exactly what she had been aiming at since she arrived in her new life, but the timing was difficult. All these interruptions ... The appointments she'd booked yesterday morning had to go off smoothly. She felt her heart lurch - she'd double-check them all, and make sure that nothing could get in the way of them and her deadlines.

That's when she saw the email. It had arrived the night before, but she'd been fussing over Marigold, still wrapped in the harmony they'd developed when she'd devoted the whole day to her. The message asked to bring this afternoon's appointment with a very busy public figure forward to this morning. And she'd missed it! Now she was seriously in the soup. She hastily replied to the email explaining that this morning had not been a possibility, and offering the next morning instead. She sat back for a moment and read what she'd written, before adding a blind copy to Joanne. Better to let her see what had happened before word got to her another way, suggesting that Clare had messed up. After that conversation when Joanne had fairly laid down the law about Clare's duties, this was not the time to disappoint her. Now she felt swamped again, as she tried to catch up with everything she'd put aside yesterday. Trying to balance all this was so hard! She had to get it working - she hated this merry-go-round she was on. She paused for a moment. She really was a very single-minded person.

She shook her head and started to calm down again and think rationally. She had been pushing her life the wrong way this last couple of years. She sat back in her chair, pensively chewing her pen as she gazed at the top of the trees she could just see out of her window. She was sure of it now – she'd been denying reality by focussing on what she wanted. She had so many years to catch up on. She'd put her ambitions on hold for so long. But perhaps Marigold had hit the nail on the head when she said that all her life contributed to who she was, and that you can't isolate your life experiences from each other.

She remembered Aidan, an old friend of hers, whose passions in life were a strange mix of cricket and liturgical music. But his day job was as a travelling salesman. He did well in his work, but saw it simply as a way to pay the bills. It was totally unconnected to everything he really wanted to spend his time on. She'd always thought it odd that he had two totally separate parts of his life, which didn't even cross, never mind work together, as she had always thought that total immersion was the only way. She guessed that rather than try and make his income from his interests, Aidan preferred to keep them as hobbies and earn money elsewhere. It wasn't the same as carving up her life the way Tabitha had done - with such disastrous results - or as Clare was trying to do. He accorded his work the time and attention it needed to be done well, and when he wasn't working he was absolutely not working! This seemed to be an unemotional division of his life, giving him plenty of time to spend with his family, uninterrupted. Of course, he had Fiona to look after the children so he could work - also without interruption. The big divide was still there, Clare smiled wryly, and she thought with a jolt that what she was basing her beliefs on had been formulated for her by a man. And what a different perspective they had on life!

At the moment what she was doing was putting everything into her work. She didn't have any other hobbies or interests. She thought back to when she was writing stories at school, then studying writing once the children were away at school. That was a hobby - well, it was her passion! And she'd turned that passion into her life, her income. Her work was all-encompassing. And she realised that in dedicating herself to this work, she had drifted away from her children - who should have been the most important things in her life! She remembered how badly she had treated Paul yesterday in the café. She'd have to ring him and put things right. Maybe Paul and Nick, and wotsisname, had become her hobbies, her diversions from the reality of her work?

It was Rollo who had first alerted her to the 'Marigold problem'. Rollo had shown that he was more attuned to Marigold than Clare was! And Marigold was showing up as a bit of a mystery to her right now. The children she thought she knew so well were growing into adults who inhabited a different world. And she felt a jolt inside when she thought how little she really knew them.

Maybe this was normal. Our children are, after all, separate beings. We bring them into the world and do our best to rear them according to our beliefs and standards. Then off they go, to discover their own beliefs, make their own standards. And yet, those beliefs inculcated into them by their upbringing can linger deep inside, as she was discovering. They can guide our decisions long after the lessons have been forgotten. A parent's shadow can be long. Generations unto generations ...

Clare thought of her own relationship with her parents. Her genius father, the famous poet, who had sacrificed his family on the altar of his art. Her mother, who had also let her down when she most needed help. How much they had influenced her life, that life she had innocently thought she was building for herself!

Since her mind had dredged up that old memory in her father's den, she had been trying to seek out and address all the places the idea had lodged in her. She was finding it had guided her all the time, like a secret satnav, while she thought she was making independent decisions. Believing what her father had told her, that she would be no good at her art if she didn't devote herself wholeheartedly to it, had caused her to stagnate creatively all those years. His idea of promoting creativity had actually stopped it entirely!

She sighed, put down her gnawed pen and walked over to the window. Even her home kept her separate from the world. Living in a city, you can pick your friends and the neighbours you talk to in a way quite impossible in the countryside of her youth, or the home of her married life, where you rubbed shoulders with the great, the humble, the good, and the not-so-good. And from growing up in wild, deep countryside, then living on a manicured estate for years, the closest she'd get to nature these days was looking at the uppermost branches of the trees waving in the wind outside her flat. Except, of course, when she stepped into Tabitha's world of long countryside walks, or visited her mother's cottage garden with its chattering chickens. She shivered and wrapped her arms round herself. She had isolated herself from her past. Why?

And the crazy thing was that she made her living from delving into other people's pasts! Her skill at questioning and digging deep had produced some of her best work. She took people gently on guided journeys through their histories, finding what had sparked their present situations. It was taking Echo back to her roots and her deep desires that had caused such a stir with that piece. Echo's honesty had shone through.

Her own deliberate isolation from her past told her she was trying to shake free of something. What was it, and how did this benefit her? She had constructed this new life with the one aim of furthering her own writing career. She hadn't planned on excising all the good from it.

And what was she losing?

Clearly she was not succeeding at keeping her work life separate from the rest of her life, as Aidan had. Her history, her family, was bursting back into it and disrupting it. She thought she'd left motherhood behind when the children had become independent, or she thought they had become so! But they would always need her - after all, look at how she was turning to Peggy! Perhaps she had an important role to play in the rest of their lives. Her own mother had come good over the last number of years. These days she was always there when she needed her. And she knew she should be there for her own children, without feeling interrupted or resentful.

She was going to have to build in time for this. She'd have to talk to Joanne, and gradually introduce the fact that she was no longer available round the clock. Her heart lurched as she thought of the email she'd just sent. Was Joanne even now reading it and noting her inefficiency and chaos? She'd enjoyed the time she'd spent with her daughter yesterday, and saw how self-centred she'd been by missing out on that. She fingered the tiny amethyst she was wearing again today. It was a cry from her daughter to be noticed, to be loved. This love was a priceless jewel. It deserved pole position in her life. She had to rebuild the relationship with her family - the intertwined relationships of Peggy, Rollo, and Marigold. And she could push aside the relationships that weren't serving her - except to bolster her ego. So she'd be saying goodbye to Paul and Nick for a start. She was surprised to find herself uttering a big sigh as she made this decision. And not a sigh of regret, but of relief. That chapter was over. True friendships were worth the world. And she had those in Tabitha, and now, increasingly, Melanie. Not to mention Nat her devoted friend on the Sports desk, who sounded so like Tabitha's old friend Gerard!

She wondered for a moment if she could salvage the friendship part of her relationship with the two guys. She did enjoy their social time together. Backtracking on her decision already! No, she was definitely finished with the affairs, but she had to be kind and considerate about it. She'd think something up before she called Paul to apologise about yesterday.

Both Tabitha and Melanie worked very hard at their chosen careers, but they still had time for "real life". They didn't have children, of course. But they were both devoted to their animals and their students. And they were such rounded and calm people! Not frantic and driven as Clare was nowadays. It had to be possible for her to work this out. Now she had clarity on what star she had been mistakenly following, it all seemed so much clearer.

She started to question if all this creativity and dedication was really worth it. But it was important for people to follow their own passions, even parents! She certainly wanted her children to follow their own desires, and to feel they were contributing to the world. She shrugged and sighed loudly.

"This won't butter me no parsnips!" she said out loud. "I have another piece to slot in to make up for Melanie's."

Melanie's postponed photoshoot was something she was really looking forward to, and she saw that this was a great instance of work and life mixing together. This gave her something to aim for!

Then - remembering how much she enjoyed her work, and how absorbing it was - she went back to her desk and got started on her next piece with renewed enthusiasm.

21

"Rhys has got better loads faster than I expected!" Melanie said excitedly on the phone a week later. "I was really hard on the poor thing, and he was barely allowed to move at all. But it's paid off! He's completely sound now, and the vet has done a thorough exam and given him the all-clear."

"Lucky you have a good vet," said Clare, after congratulating her on her determination.

"Oh, he's a specialist. He works a lot with greyhounds and racehorses, especially jumpers. So he knows exactly what all these injuries are, and how to fix them. He's quite a drive away from me, but so worth it."

"Yes, Jonathan has one of those specialist vets for his racehorses - worth his weight in gold. We all seem to specialise these days - you with your dancing, Tabitha with her kids, me with sensitive journalism!" She smiled. Melanie's mood was so much lighter now than it had been when she first broke the news about Rhys' injury, and Clare was pleased to hear the relief in her friend's voice.

Harriet found a space in her calendar and they were able to get the photoshoot re-fixed very quickly. So on the day Clare was delighted to arrive and see Tabitha's car in the drive next to Melanie's battered white van. This was going to be fun!

"We have a quorum!" she laughed as she went into the warm kitchen, to be greeted by Rhys, even getting a tentative sniff with a very long neck from Heidi.

"Day off today," said Tabitha, smugly. "And what better way to spend it?"

"Lucky you," Melanie looked up from her coffee-making duties, "I've got a couple of sessions this afternoon, so I'll have to dash once Harriet's done. I'm sorry I can't offer you lunch .."

"That's fine," chorused Clare and Tabitha.

"You got your dogs with you, Tabs?" said Clare, turning to her friend.

"You really need to ask?" she smiled.

Clare laughed saying, "Perhaps we could go for a walk together after the shoot?"

"Love that!" agreed Tabitha. Clare smiled warmly, and smiled inwardly too. She'd got the interim piece finished for Joanne who had surprised her (as she so often did, with her unpredictability) by being very understanding about the missed appointment. She'd spoken to Paul who didn't seem to be much bothered - there were plenty more fish in the sea for him. Marigold was getting steadily better with days at a time going by without tears: things seemed to be evening out nicely. Clare was juggling lots of different things and managing to keep all the balls in the air. It was satisfying, and she felt better about life than she had for a while. The company of her two friends always seemed to have a good effect on her.

Shortly after, Harriet arrived to find a happy and eager group awaiting her. After some discussion with Clare on what she was looking for, and ensuring Harriet was well coffee-ed up, they all went to the barn where Harriet worked out positions, backgrounds, and lighting. Harriet asked Melanie to run through a couple of samples so she could decide on her angles and focus and lots of other technical stuff that she adjusted on the many dials and knobs of her cameras.

"Why so many cameras?" asked Melanie.

"They're mostly using different lenses. Zooms, macros, it's as easy to have the lenses already fitted on separate cameras than try to change them over mid-session.

"I'd like to take some portraits of you outside in natural light too, Melanie - I'd love to get the sun catching your red hair. These surroundings are so beautiful. As is your kitchen - very characteristic, cosy. Maybe some pictures of you with your dogs round the Aga? With all those rosettes on the wall just in frame?"

So they got to work, Clare and Tabitha keeping well out of the way of the action, but applauding loudly after each take, to keep Melanie focussed on her dog and not become self-conscious about the photographer. Harriet was as amazed as Clare had been when she watched the handler and her dog becoming so absorbed, the beauty of the dog's actions reflected in Melanie's fluid movement. When they squinted at the little thumbnails in Harriet's laptop, Clare could see several that would make great additions to her story. Harriet zoomed in on a few, and showed the concentration on Rhys's face as he worked, as well as a lighter shot of the connection between the two of them, Melanie smiling with love, and Rhys smiling right back.

"I never knew dogs could actually smile," Clare pointed to one of the images. Tabitha and Melanie exchanged glances and theatrical sighs.

"I'm always telling you," said Tabitha, "dogs are people too!"

The photoshoot went off without a hitch. Clare admired Harriet's skill at quietly getting just what she wanted out of her subjects, hardly impinging on them at all - just gently guiding now and then. Melanie was surprised to find how much she'd enjoyed it. "Come on, Melanie, you're a seasoned performer!" Tabitha had teased her. Clare was relieved to know this article was at last ready to turn in, to redeem her somewhat with Joanne. And she was going to be rewarded with a bit of time with her friend.

It was a bit later when Harriet had packed up all her gear and left, promising to let Clare have all the thumbnails the next day - and Melanie had to shoo them out so she could go herself - that Tabitha and Clare got the dogs out and set off on a walk together, with cries of "Bye Rhys! Bye Heidi!" Tabitha knew these surroundings well, and was able to choose a dry path to accommodate Clare's townie footwear.

They set off down a grassy footpath before entering a large stand of trees of every kind. The canopy above them was alive with bird and squirrel activity, as the forest denizens were stocking up on food for the winter ahead.

"Gerard's daughter is back home now," said Tabitha, as Esme ran ahead with the big puppy. "He's back at work, so I have some time to myself today."

"Wonderful news. Terrible thing for a parent to have happen. Thank goodness she's ok."

"Gerard's convinced it's all down to his wife knowing immediately that something was very wrong. 'Mothers always know,' he says."

Clare was silent, as she thought of how she seemed to have completely failed her daughter. She was doing her best to put things right now. But things had got so bad before Marigold was forced to turn to her mother in her wretchedness. That would never happen between Melanie and her father, she felt sure.

"So how's it going with you," asked Tabitha quietly.

"I've been thinking."

"That sounds bad!" she laughed.

Clare smiled at her friend. "I've been questioning everything. I don't know if everything is happening at once, or I'm just noticing things which have been staring me in the face all along. You know, like if you want a red car, all you see is red cars everywhere. They were always there, you just didn't notice them."

Cariad lolloped back to Tabitha, poked her leg with her nose, looked up at her with shining eyes, then raced off again to catch Esme. "See her smile there?" asked Tabitha.

"Oh, sorry, I missed it." Clare was deep in her thoughts now. "You see, I thought ... I thought that to do justice to my art I had to focus on it completely. That I could only work effectively if I had no other pull on my time, my emotions."

She scuffed through some early Autumn leaves that had been blown in a spiral into a small heap on the path. Tabitha listened without inter-rupting as they walked.

"An old memory came back to me. It was when my father was telling me that if I didn't devote myself to my creative work full-time, without distraction from people - boyfriends, family - I was wasting my time. That's why I did almost nothing while the children were young. It seems so stupid now."

"I'm sure rearing the children and running that huge house must have been a full-time job," offered Tabitha.

"Yes, that's true. But if I'd really wanted to, I could have made time somewhere, in the corners of the day. Other people do. People who work full-time manage to paint, or write books, or sing ... I had it in my head that I could only do one thing or the other. That any work I did would be sub-standard if it were diluted by real life." She spread her arms out. "That to be creative you had to be self-centred." She turned towards Tabitha who was looking pensive, "Real life can't interfere with the muse."

She kicked another pile of leaves. "It fed into my perfectionism. That if I couldn't do it wholeheartedly, I shouldn't do it at all. I suppose it was an escape clause. To avoid trying and running the chance of failing. Maybe that's why I avoided it for so long?"

The dogs came bursting out of a thicket, checked their people were keeping up, then ran off ahead of them again, noses to the ground.

"I suppose after twenty years I was getting more and more dissatisfied with family life. Frustrated. Winding socks and cooking dinners wears thin after a while. I thought that happiness lay in stopping denying my creative side. I'd have to be self-centred, as so many men are in pursuit of their chosen path. I suppose that's why I took up with men I could keep at a distance, men who were already committed elsewhere - or who would never commit. I could enjoy a bit of a social life without it impinging on my work. But I'm not sure it works like that.

"And you know what?" she stopped and turned to Tabitha. "When I made my grand gesture and left Jonathan, it turned out he'd been carrying on with Aisling for years without me having a clue. The kids knew. But I didn't. It kind of made my bid for freedom rather empty. He barely noticed."

Tabitha reached out a hand and squeezed her friend's shoulder as they carried on walking again.

"I think you're measuring by the wrong standard," said Tabitha after a few steps. "We may both be human beings, living on the same planet, but men are not the same as women. They've been brought up and taught totally differently. We've been socialised to serve, to keep our place, to be in the background, keeping the wheels turning. And the changes that are taking place now in society are massive. People's ideas are so different from what they were when we were children.

"It's human nature to take something if it's given to you," she went on, warming to her theme. "To maintain the status quo if it works in your favour. The menfolk aren't bad. They just *are*." She turned and looked at Clare, who felt her brave face beginning to crumple. "And it's human nature, in the main, to accept the status quo and be at the mercy of it. But it doesn't have to be like that."

She peeled another strip of bark off the twig Cariad had pressed into her hand on her last drive-by.

"You were there for me when I needed help. I was in the grip of something similar to what you're going through now. Having to face something I'd been pushing away for years. The least I can do is return the favour! You'd got everything going just as you thought you wanted it, and Marigold turning up in crisis has completely flittered your life. It's lying in pieces round you. Time for you to find the valuable pieces and re-assemble your life in a way it can really work for you."

"I wake up in the night," Clare said, and waited while Tabitha checked what Cariad was digging at in a pile of leaves. Satisfied it wasn't alive or dangerous, she turned back to Clare as they walked on again. "And I can't get back to sleep again. I've just got this vague feeling of worry, of anxiety. But the trouble is, I don't know what it is I'm worried about! My mind keeps trying to fit it to things - and you can always find worries in your life, things you've forgotten, things you've still got to do, things you're not sure how to do - but there's this sort of low rumble of anxiety. Of course, with Marigold here I know things aren't right. But I just can't put my finger on it, and I feel as if I'm groping in the dark to find out what the trouble is and what's worrying me. Until I can find that I don't know that I can do anything about it." Tears trickled down her cheeks.

They walked in silence for a while, Clare blowing her nose on her now-damp tissue before continuing, "I have a feeling what may be bothering me is that Marigold is trying to follow in my footsteps. She perceives me as the great role-model, following my passion without need for family. I don't know if that's played into this break-up with Tiernan, or whether it's the other way round, and the split has prompted her to look at what I'm doing and follow that path. Either way I feel I'm letting her down. I can't win ..."

"Now that's not the strong Clare I know and love!" said Tabitha hotly. "Don't let yourself slide down into feeling helpless. You're not, and you know it. But I do understand," she relented a little in her tone of voice, "I get why you're feeling this way. It's all been a lot to happen in a short time. And after you'd done so well with your breakthrough piece, people beginning to notice you. I mean the one about that starlet in trouble."

"Echo."

"Yes, that one. You know I don't keep up with pop gossip! But even I overheard the older girls at the Junior Academy talking about it, and how they'd read in their Mum's magazine that she was really nice underneath it all."

The dogs were closer to them now, walking more slowly, and responding happily to Tabitha dishing out some treats to them.

"You have a gift. You did that great piece about me - even I learned something about myself from it!" she laughed as she turned towards Clare. "And I don't think you'd be able to write as you do if you hadn't experienced the life you've had. Just supposing you'd heeded your father's advice, like you always used to say you would back at school."

"I wanted to," interrupted Clare, "but nature had other things in store for me." They both smiled. "Ah, we were babes in the wood back then," Clare laughed, as she reflected on Tabitha's words.

"Well, supposing that hadn't happened, you hadn't had to get married, and you'd followed your plan. I don't think you'd be able to understand people half as well as you do. It's through living life that we get to understand it."

"Yes, that experience certainly helped me understand the dynamic between Echo and her mother. Yes, what you're saying is true. And you know what? It's exactly what Marigold said to me last week. In some ways she has such an old head on her shoulders."

"Thanks!" laughed Tabitha as she accepted the new twig Esme had brought her, then signalled her little dog to spin once on the spot, before tossing it away into the woods beside the path for her to hunt down amongst the thousands of similar sticks on the forest floor. Cariad found it almost instantly, and trotted along beside them proudly displaying it, as Tabitha continued: "But we do have to be aware, critical, as we live our life. That's where I went so wrong. I just accepted everything that happened to me as if it were divinely ordained. But as you well know, it's what we believe about ourselves that makes the world happen as it does. It was when my friends - including you!" she turned to face Clare again, "when they hammered it into me that it was up to me to change every-thing, that I made my new life."

They had reached the edge of the wood and looked up at some tele-graph poles with wires leading to a couple of cottages. The wires were covered with hundreds of busy, noisy swallows, assembling to prepare for their long journey south together.

"I need to get rid of the perfectionism, this damned single-minded-ness," agreed Clare, shoving the no-longer-needed tissue deep into her pocket. "I need to start making some sensible decisions. As always, Tabitha, you're so right."

"No. Not 'as always'. There was a time when I was far deeper in the murk than you. So much more invested in what I believed, and which was so completely wrong!"

"Well, as always you are a tower of strength. An inspiration. Maybe I'll bless the day Marigold rocked up at my door. I told her that only last night. I wasn't sure if I was telling the truth or not. Maybe I was. Maybe it'll be the start of a more even, more fulfilling life."

Tabitha smiled encouragingly at her friend, as they linked arms and enjoyed the beautiful woodland as they walked back along the path to Melanie's home and their cars.

The walk had been cathartic. Clare had been wallowing in the thought that her relationships were all shallow - that she was keeping everyone at arm's length: not just the new men in her life, but everyone. Now she realised she did have friends to whom she was important. And they were the constants in her life. Like her family. It was time to let them all in, and enjoy this rich life together.

22

Clare returned home feeling shriven, fulfilled, hopeful, validated. It had been an important day. A day of moment. She had at last made sense of what was happening in her life, and she had ideas on how to move forward. As she ascended the stairs and fished her keys out of her pocket, she remembered turning the corner at the top of the stairs to see the dark shape she'd found at her door a few weeks earlier. She felt a wave of anguish deep inside, not only at the memory, but at the knowledge that despite the pleasant outing she and Marigold had shared, she still had a sad daughter to deal with. This nursing lark really wasn't her *forte!* But she took a deep breath, relaxed her shoulders and her face, and let herself in.

She could feel the blast of warmth in the flat as she opened the door. Marigold must have turned the heating up. She put her things down on the kitchen worktop and called her.

"In here, Mum," came a muffled voice from Marigold's room. She went in, to find her daughter huddled in bed, hugging her knees to her. "Got something to tell you, Mummy," she said, pulling herself up in bed, revealing a pale face with smudged eyes and sweat-tangled curls of hair. "Tell you what, can you put the kettle on while I get up? I fancy a coffee. Got anything nice to go with it?"

Clare went obediently to the kitchen and started rummaging in the cupboards for biscuits and bars, clinking mugs and cafetière, making those reassuring noises that presaged a comforting and refreshing hot drink. Her daughter was asking for food! This had to be a good sign of recovery.

And when Marigold emerged from her room, she looked somehow fresher, more hopeful, more ... Marigold. Her hair was brushed and bouncy, her clothes seemed to fit her better, rather than hang lifelessly on her. She took her mug and a laden plate of biscuits and sat in an armchair, motioning Clare to do the same.

"You look so much brighter, Marigold! Are you feeling better?"

"A thousand times better." She munched a chocolate biscuit. "I have to make a confession." Clare saw that Marigold found it hard to look directly at her, but then with a conscious effort she turned her face to her mother.

"I lied. I'm sorry, but I lied to you." She hurried on, "I felt cornered," averting her gaze once more, "I felt I had to." She looked straight at Clare again. "I *was* pregnant." A pause. "But I'm not any more, thank heavens. I've had an abortion."

Clare gasped. "Marigold! When? Are you ok? How ... ?" she tailed off, trying to absorb this news – such a momentous event and she hadn't had an inkling.

"Today. When I heard you'd fixed your long day out today, I knew this was the moment. The well woman place have been great. They wouldn't let me rush into it. They talked to me loads about it all. Told me all the pros and cons, possible side-effects, knock-on effects later. And they gave me the space I needed to make my decision. And I'm happy about it. Relieved, now!" she gave a smile that Clare hadn't seen since she'd arrived. The smile changed her from being a problem daughter to being the child Clare had always known, and loved.

"But why lie? Why couldn't you tell me?" Clare was beginning to feel resentment flooding over her, her cheeks flushing. She felt deceived, and could feel the prickings of anger.

"I really wanted to, Mum! But I was afraid you'd go all religious on me."

"Me? Religious?!"

"Well, culturally religious, perhaps. I didn't know what you'd think. I know you went ahead and had Rollo, married Dad. But I didn't know whether you'd ever considered abortion - how possible it was then. And I was determined. I felt I couldn't take the risk. I didn't want you to try and stop me. I had to do this on my own."

"You can get abortions in Ireland these days," said Clare thoughtfully. "Why did you need to come here for it?"

"I was over the time limit. And, honestly, I felt the need of a bit of mothering," she gave Clare a brave smile. "Even if I could have had it there, I needed you."

"Oh darling! And I've been so preoccupied. I thought you were having some kind of breakdown over Tiernan, and I really didn't know how to help you. I hoped that counselling and time would heal you. I had no idea ... Now I feel so bad!" Her anger was now turning to wretchedness and guilt.

"No, Mum. It's my fault for not telling you. I hated lying to you. And to Amma. But I was afraid. I felt alone."

Clare wrung her hands in anguish at hearing this. She had been so completely focussed on herself that she'd failed her daughter in her time of need. She should have known! She should have been aware! She had been so wrapped up in her own affairs for so long she was becoming self-centred, her priorities distorted.

"Rollo has been great," added Marigold, taking another mouthful of chocolate biscuit, and sounding positively chirpy. "He's been telling me to make my own decision. Not worry about what anyone else may think."

"The rascal! So that's what he meant by one plus one equalling three ..." said Clare, the light dawning. "I'm so glad you had someone you could confide in, Marigold. And I feel terrible that it wasn't me." She looked earnestly at her daughter, who now seemed transformed as she helped herself to yet another chocolate biscuit.

"I'm so relieved that one plus one are *not* equalling three!" grinned Marigold. "There is no 'one plus one' for a start. Tiernan legged it the minute I told him about the 'three'. I can't forgive him for that - ever - specially when he'd been vowing undying love to me a few weeks before.

He showed his true colours." She turned to her mother. "But I knew that I could depend on you, Mummy - just not tell you till after the deed was done."

"You've followed your heart and made a decision that was right for you. You can't do better than that." Clare took a sip of her coffee, still warm enough in the heat of the flat. "I don't actually have any strong views about abortion either way. I'm not going to start blaming you. It's clearly something to avoid if possible - a last resort I suppose. But what about you, now? Do you have to rest for ages? What do you need?"

"There's info here," Marigold produced a slim booklet from the pocket of her cardigan and handed it to Clare. "There's what to do if any of that nasty list of symptoms appear. But they tell me they're very unusual, and I could probably go back to work tomorrow."

"No chance," said Clare firmly, taking the booklet and starting to leaf through it. "You've been through enough in the run-up to this, never mind an operation and anaesthetic to recover from too. You'll stay here and take it easy for a few days at least." Marigold's face relaxed as she leant back in her chair. "And how did you manage it? You surely didn't walk back here?" Clare looked up with a shocked face.

"Remember when you gave me money for a taxi in case I felt floppy when I first went out? I kept it and used that. Don't worry, I'm following what they say."

"How many pads are you getting through?" Clare asked anxiously, glancing up from the book where she was looking at 'excessive bleeding' under the symptoms list.

"Less than they say. It's all going as they said it should. I'll tell you if I start getting through them, promise. I don't want to bleed to death in the night!" Marigold made an effort to make light of it all. "I'd hate to have done this on my own," she added with a coy smile.

Clare gazed at her and smiled softly back. "Tell me, where did you get the money from? Wasn't it expensive? Did you ask your father?"

"No, I didn't want to ask Dad. There's this charity in Ireland," replied Marigold. "They're brilliant. They gave me the money - or rather, they paid it straight to the Centre. I came over on the boat and train, so I managed that ok."

"Then we must pay them back. Give me the details tomorrow and I'll write out a cheque. And here, I'll give you the money to fly home: no boats or trains. You need to look after yourself, get fully fit and healthy again. These things take time ..."

Clare was beginning to cycle through all the emotions - shock, shame .. guilt. She wasn't enjoying any of them, and guilt least of all. She used to have a hard line approach to this 'sin' when she was under the influence of her school and upbringing, but she had long since learnt through others' experiences that it wasn't as cut and dried - as simple and straight-forward - as the male powers-that-be would like to think. She firmly believed that everyone's life was their own, that they could decide on their own path in life, their own sexuality, and whether or not they would choose to rear a child. Yet it was still a shock. The finality of it ... It would take her a little while to adjust to this new situation, and leave the recent troubled past behind.

"I'm actually able to see forward again, already." It was as if Marigold had been following her train of thought. "I'm beginning to itch to get back to my work. This has been a nightmare. I'm so glad it's over and I can get on with my life again. And won't I be more careful in future!"

"That's wonderful to hear. You're sounding more like your old self. Well, you can stay here as long as you need." Clare was pleased to notice that she was able to extend the invitation with no feeling of resentment at all, now that the mystery was resolved and Marigold seemed back to normal. "And I'll ring Joanne and cancel tomorrow's meeting so I can keep an eye on you - this list of symptoms looks serious. You shouldn't be alone - I'll be watching over you. I've got plenty I can do from home."

Clare took a drink of her coffee. "And I feel so much better now too," she added. "Now it's all explained. Oh my poor baby! You'll never have to hide anything from me ever again. Here," she said, seeing a grimace of pain pass over Marigold's face as she pressed her hands on her belly. "You're getting these cramps they talk about. Why don't you go back to bed. I'll bring a hot water bottle for your tum. Is there anything else you need?"

"That's a good idea. They've given me painkillers to take - think I'll take a couple more. I do feel tired now. It's the emotional upheaval, I think. I didn't know whether I'd be covered in guilt afterwards," she said, getting up carefully from the chair. "But I'm not." She smiled and bent to give Clare a kiss. "I knew I could count on you, when it came down to it."

As Clare went to organise the hot water bottle, she felt reassured that she wasn't as bad as she'd been thinking. "For Marigold to say that, I must have been doing something right," she thought. "Maybe I can manage to do things better - and everything doesn't have to be perfect?"

23

Marigold slept well for a few hours, and awoke once more hungry. Clare was pleasantly surprised to find herself switching back happily to her motherhood role, happy to feed up her ailing daughter. Her child needed her, needed to get back to full health, and she was happy to support her. She found her resentment of this burden evaporating. She could feel big shifts as her priorities rearranged themselves in a pleasing way. And in the place of that resentment she felt the love that had been buried under her busyness all along. It warmed her heart. It warmed her soul.

The conflict between her work-life and her real life was ebbing away. Clare rang Joanne early the next morning, to assure her that her projects were all in hand but she couldn't make their meeting. She rehearsed what she was going to say, delivered it, and waited with trepidation to hear how it was received. She was relieved to find herself standing firm as - not unexpectedly - Joanne ranted at her. So when her Editor found she was making no headway with her valuable writer, she softened and said, "I've seen Harriet's pictures of the dog thing. They're very striking. Once you've sorted the captions we'll be able to put that one to bed. You're getting an extra page this time."

"Ooh, great!" replied Clare enthusiastically. "You know, Joanne," she went on, "I really feel like I'm hitting my stride with this article. I've got great ideas for the follow-up on Echo too, and I'm turning ideas round in my mind for the other ones we chose."

They discussed Clare's revised schedule animatedly for a short while before they rang off, both eager to busy themselves with their work.

It didn't take Clare long to select the photos she wanted for the article. Several of them jumped off the page of thumbnails! Apart from the one of Melanie and Rhys smiling at each other, there was a lovely one of Melanie looking pensive in dappled light amongst her trees, the sun glinting on her red curls. And she chose a small version of a cosy, homely image of her and her dogs gathered round the Aga, Melanie with a coffee mug in hand, both dogs looking up at her expectantly. A bit more polishing and the whole thing would be ready for publication. She was pleased with the almost-finished piece, feeling that she'd done justice to the complex character behind Melanie's simple love of animals. That would keep Joanne happy while she took this time off!

And her next task was to do a bit of research into what symptoms and side-effects she had to look out for in Marigold. So far she seemed to be recovering fast, and the emotional collapse that Clare feared hadn't yet hit her. There was still time for that to happen. But right now, Marigold was so much more herself. Perhaps she was right, and the nightmare was over.

They had plenty of time to talk to each other that day. And Clare, revelling in the honesty between them now, told her about her own, similar, crisis, all those years ago, when she had found herself pregnant with Rollo, with little idea what to do.

"Yes, they did have abortion back then. Well, it's always been there - but it used to be 'back-street abortion' and was dirty and dangerous and only for the completely desperate. There was still a lot of stigma attached, even once it was legalised. I was living in England - still at school - and technically I could have had an abortion, but I actually didn't consider it. Catholic upbringing, I guess. And I was in love with your father - and he loved me too, though he may not have wanted to marry me if this hadn't happened, who knows? So when he stepped forward and offered to 'make an honest woman' of me, it seemed the right thing to do.

"You see Dad - your Ampa - darkly disapproved of me consorting with a West Brit, a member of the aristocracy, and a proddydog to boot!"

"Proddydog?" echoed Marigold.

"Rude Catholic term for protestants - don't they use that any more? I *am* out of touch! The fewer insults people hurl at each other the better ... And Mum followed his lead. It's strange because she's not Irish - she's an English blow-in. I always felt that I had a foot in both camps. But I had no support there," she added sadly. "I had no idea what else I could do."

"But I thought you got on well with Amma?"

"I do, now. Poor woman has been trying to make up for this ever since. And she adores you two, as you know! You see, had I known your plight, I would have supported you. I like to think I'd have supported whatever decision you made. But I can see why you wanted to keep your cards close to your chest. I may have tried to influence you one way or the other. I get that. All in all, I'm glad you lied to me!" Clare peered into her almost-empty coffee mug ruminatively, then added brightly, "And it's good that you made your own decision, on your own, that you'll be able to live with for the rest of your life. No blame. No regrets. That should not be anyone else's business but yours."

With their new-found *camaraderie*, Marigold began to get animated as they talked long through the morning about her hopes and aspirations.

"I love what I'm studying, Mum, it's so rewarding. Amazing what our forebears thought and believed. And the way they gave expression to it in their art is astonishing. Such beautiful artefacts! We go to a lot of these ancient archaeological sites as part of the syllabus - I love it. One day we'll be visiting neolithic burial mounds, and another day we'll be trekking up a holy mountain, studying *crannogs* or *clocháns*."

"Clock-whats?"

"*Clocháns* - those little beehive huts for hermit monks all over the place in Kerry, *you* remember! - or we go looking for fairy circles: circular clumps of trees," Clare nodded as she listened to her daughter enthuse, not wanting to break the spell. "You see them as islands in fields: farmers preserve them, they plough round them. They don't want to annoy the fairies," she smiled happily. "And I want to keep this heritage alive, not pickled in aspic, only found in dusty books and museums. The music and poetry people make now are so heavily influenced by it." She got more excited and enthusiastic as she spoke. Clare couldn't see these things - her people's history - as very relevant to today. But she loved her daughter's dedication to it. Just as Rollo was studying scientific marvels of the future Clare couldn't begin to understand, Marigold was studying cultural marvels of the past in a way which also eluded her. Clare herself very much lived in the present. So all through the day she encouraged her daughter to talk, to unburden whatever she wanted.

She heard about Tiernan, and the doomed relationship. At one stage she pointed out the wisdom in the well woman leaflet on the available methods of contraception. Marigold reached for the leaflet and scanned the list.

"Number Six doesn't work," she said with a rueful grin, tossing the book back on the table. They both laughed conspiratorially.

They talked about her other friends at university. Who she could easily spend time with without disturbing her studies. While she had had the big love affair with Tiernan, her other friends had taken a back seat, along with her studies. Her summer exam grades had not been what she'd expected.

"I'm never going to be caught like that again," she averred fiercely. "It was so stupid, to sacrifice my studies and my friends for an infatuation. This is what I was born to do, and this is what I *will* do."

"So long as you keep room for all the things in your life that are also important to you - your friends, the fun you have with them ..." Clare chipped in, anxious to redress some of the influence she'd had on her daughter's priorities.

After eating an astonishingly large amount of lunch, Marigold decided to go out for a brief walk on her own. "These cramps are settling a bit, and I think stretching a leg will help. I know you've got things to do Mum - I'll just go to the park and back, spend some time on my own, okay? I won't go far. And yes," she added quickly, seeing Clare's expression, "I *have* got my phone!" as she waved it in the air.

"Take some money from my purse, just in case," said Clare firmly.

"Thanks - I've only got Euros."

"Oh, and have you thought about Amma?" Clare asked moments later, Marigold's hand on the door handle.

"She'll have to know, I guess," thought Marigold. "But won't it upset her? Great-grandchild and all that?"

"I think she'll accept your own decision over your own life."

"Can you tell her, Mum? I'm not sure I could cope with it if she .."

"I know, 'went all religious on you'! Ok. I'll clear the path. But you will probably have to talk to her yourself some time."

So Clare grabbed the opportunity to ring Peggy. She had to be told, if only to settle her mind, and confirm that she was right. And she wasn't sure how she'd receive the news, and didn't want to risk Marigold walking into a row.

"I *knew* she was pregnant," said Peggy triumphantly. "Just *knew* it."

"And do you mind?" asked Clare.

"Well, it's not the best thing to have happened. But she's made her own decision, and we can respect that."

Clare drew in her breath sharply.

"Yes, I know what you're thinking, Clare. But that was then, and this is now. I'm a better person, a sadder and a wiser bear. What Marigold needs is our love, not our condemnation, whatever we may think about the whole thing. I'd love to see her. Would she like to come up here to convalesce, do you think?"

"She's actually doing really well. Eating like a horse again. Lively, looking forward. She's a different beast from when she fetched up on my doorstep a few weeks ago. But sure, give her a ring and ask her."

After this, she called Rollo. He'd texted her asking how things were - he was obviously in touch with Marigold.

"I'm glad it's all worked out ok," he said, flicking his hair out of his eyes. "It's absurd that two people can cause something and only one of them has to carry the can. I didn't want to influence her decision - but I did want her to know we'd support her. Well, I knew you would, in the end."

"What do you mean, 'in the end'?"

"Well, I agreed with her. Best to keep it to herself till she was ready."

"I should be glad you two look out for each other, even if you are ganging up on me. Gives me hope for the future. One day I won't be here ..."

"Long way off yet, Mum! But what about Dad? Has anyone told him?"

"I think Marigold can do that in her own time. After all, it doesn't change anything. I don't think he'll be bothered much by the abortion, and he does love you two. He's really busy in the lead-up to the *Arc* at the moment, so I'm sure he'll appreciate not having had to deal with this. It's all done now. So he doesn't need to bother his barney over it." She thought for a moment, then added, "I'm glad you're a more modern male," and they ended the call, both smiling.

Clare's last call was to Echo. She'd had an email from her, saying how much she appreciated her insights and what it had done for her publicity, how it had turned the public back in her favour. She asked Clare to ring her, and she was on this call when Marigold returned, rosy-cheeked and contented.

"So I wondered if you'd like to come up again. I've got some friends who'd love to meet you - other showbiz people. I know it's a bit of a trek for you, so I thought a lunch party would work. What do you think?"

Clare was very happy with this plan. She'd get some more interviews out of this for sure, and she'd enjoy meeting Echo again, learning a bit more about the interesting person behind all the glitz and show - she did genuinely like her. Such talent came at a cost - a cost so many didn't realise till it was too late. Echo was in fact a shining example, wise beyond her years.

"I'd love that," Clare replied, and they fixed a date for the following week.

"Off on your social whirl again, Mum?" asked Marigold, as Clare pressed the button on the phone and tossed it on her desk. "I won't be stopping you now."

"Well, I've just had an idea," Clare turned to face her. "Amma would love to see you and wondered if you'd like to stay with her to convalesce."

"I don't need to convalesce!" said Marigold. "I'm physically fine."

"I know, I'm just passing on her offer."

"How did she take it?" asked Marigold, biting her lip.

"Surprisingly well, actually. She really just wants the best for you, and is not going to let her opinion or anyone else's stand in the way this time round. But, you see, I'm going out that direction next week for work - that's what I was just fixing. And I could drop you at Peggy's on the way and fetch you on the way back. It's a lunch-party, so it would only be a few hours. What do you think?"

"That's a great idea, Mum! I can see her and put her mind at rest, and ... escape again," she grinned.

Clare felt a warmth in this collaboration, this scheming with her daughter, that she hadn't felt for a couple of years. She smiled back warmly. Parts of her life were slipping comfortably into place again. Things were looking up. She felt freer than she had done since she started her new life.

24

Marigold was improving visibly by the day. Clare was so pleased to have her lively daughter back again. They sorted out the moneys for the charity that had financed the operation, and Clare gave them a generous donation over and above what they'd paid out. She realised how essential this service was for desperate women who had nowhere else to turn. There was an article in this for her too. A way to get people to look past their own opinions and beliefs and see it from the other end of the spectrum. She wasn't going to venture into the thorns and try and change people's minds over what they thought right and wrong - she was not a campaigner and had no strong views either way herself - just get them to consider the 'sinner' rather than the 'sin'. Perhaps get them to focus their energies on education - especially of the male half of the problem, as Rollo had hinted! - instead of condemnation. Things hadn't changed much there in thousands of years.

There was a lot of anger and noise round this subject. But what it boiled down to for her was a young, frightened, girl who felt alone. That could never be right! Her usual habit of living in the present without the shadows of the past looming over her was an approach that really helped Clare at this time.

They fell into an easy life together while Marigold worked on catching up with her studies and making plans for her return to Ireland. She busied herself doing the shopping and some of the cooking, even baking a cake. She had booked a flight for the day after her visit to her grandmother, and was clearly full of vigour and raring to go. Clare had given a lot of thought to her daughter's words about how she was going to single-mindedly pursue her vocation. It had hit her when she'd first said it, and it was hitting her harder with each passing day.

"I'm going to be like Ampa. Like you," Marigold had said a couple of days before. "I'm going to devote myself to this. I've tried love, and it doesn't work. I know what I can trust. I know I have something to offer the world, and I'm going to be sure to do it. I'm going to follow your lead!"

The rumblings of misgivings had alerted Clare. But then had not been the time to destabilise her daughter by arguing with her over her grand plan. She felt firmly that this was not an inheritance Marigold should take up. Clare had pushed the discomfort down and carried on encouraging Marigold to talk. And she had learnt more about her work, her mission, and her friends.

Clare saw, so clearly now, that she had been following the wrong path. That was one thing - ruining her own life - but influencing her daughter to follow the same wrong road was terrible! The messages she'd received so early from her now-dead father had dictated her last couple of years, all without her realising it. She had internalised these messages and taken them as gospel truth. She hadn't questioned them. Just thought they were reality! And she thought of how it had led her away from some of the things she truly valued and towards a life where her integrity was being compromised. She had been blind to this as she pursued what she thought was real, when it was in fact just an idea planted into her young mind by someone else.

She'd been basing her life on what someone else thought. For someone who felt herself to be an independent thinker, this was a painful revelation to her! She had to look inside herself and find what else she'd accepted as truth which was simply something handed down, by school, perhaps, as well as her family. Children are so impressionable! So easy to mould. Wasn't it the Jesuits who had said, 'Give me a child till the age of seven and I will give you the man'? As always when she met a challenge, she started to dig down and dissect the problem. It had always been her way of dealing with the world, to rationalise it so she could master it. But first you needed to know where to look!

We are so vulnerable when young. And we're brought up to believe everything put before us by our all-powerful parents, and their sidekicks-in-arms the teachers. Until we hit teenage and start kicking over the traces. Then we often go to the other extreme and throw the baby out with the bathwater. Baby. Perhaps if she'd been less preoccupied she could have saved this baby? But she dismissed that thought as soon as it arrived. It was not her baby to save. Marigold had to lead her own life, and not have it derailed forever by a single mistake. And what was her mistake? Believing the avowals of love from someone she was in love with. And trusting that method no.6 would work! She wasn't a bad person, just young and foolish, with a perfectly-functioning body.

So Clare needed to find out just what message Marigold was taking from her own behaviour. She needed to make sure she made her own decisions in this regard, and not follow blindly a trail that Clare now saw was wrong. Marigold had already struck out on her own by not following her mother into motherhood, but there were other influences that needed to be examined. Influences she was probably as unaware of as Clare had been of her father's words all those years ago. Words which had crystallised in her head into a belief which had governed her whole life.

So when Marigold came back from her walk, fresh-faced and pink-cheeked from the cold October air, Clare asked her to put the kettle on. Marigold chattered as she put away her purchases from the supermarket.

"I thought we could have these shrimps for lunch," she said happily. "I got a baguette to go with them. I'll leave the change here," she added, clattering some coins and a screwed-up note onto the worktop.

She brought the steaming coffee mugs over to her mother's table.

"How's 'Melanie', Mum? All done?"

"Yep - it's scheduled for two weeks out. I've got someone else to see this week, and I hope to get some useful leads from Echo's lunch. It's all happening for me at the moment!"

"You're the saviour of the downtrodden," laughed Marigold. "I think it's marvellous how you've dedicated yourself to helping others in this way."

"I wanted to talk to you about that," started Clare slowly, settling back in her chair. "You said you want to dedicate yourself to your work. That sounds great, admirable. But I'm concerned that you're thinking you have to eschew friendship, love, and normal life in order to do that.

"You see," she said quickly, leaning forward, as Marigold opened her mouth to respond, "that's what I thought. That's what held me back all the time you were small. I felt that I had to achieve perfection, and that diluting my work with child-rearing was going to result in poor work, second-rate stuff not worth bothering with. That's why I held off till you and Rollo were both settled in your chosen studies, then I flipped the switch and dedicated myself wholeheartedly to my new work. And this is what you're seeing. I think that you're thinking you have to be single-minded to succeed." She held up her hand as Marigold wanted to speak, and continued doggedly.

"But I can see now that that's a form of perfectionism. It's a nonsense! We can never reach perfection, so using it as an excuse is crazy."

"But I feel I have work to do, Mum," Marigold jumped in as Clare paused for effect. "Something important that I can do. What's wrong with that?"

"Nothing at all - absolutely nothing! As long as you don't make the same mistake I did, and divide your life up into compartments. I wasted years by not pursuing my vocation while you were small. And then I wasted another couple of years denying my family - my whole history - and focussing only on work.

"It's taken you coming here, your over-riding need, to make me see the nonsense in this! Our lives have to be an integrated whole. One part feeds the other. I was rejecting those who loved me and wasting time with those who don't much care. You have to find what's right for you, what your heart tells you, then stick to that."

"Wow, Mum. That's an impassioned speech. Are you saying I did something wrong?"

"No. No, I'm not saying that. What happened, happened. And

you've dealt with it. What I'm worried about is you unconsciously following what I'm doing, how your grandfather lived his life. You have to find your own thing. Never mind the fact that I've been wrong. I've misled you. I don't want you to labour under a misapprehension all your life. Miss out on things which you should have." She reached for her mug. "It used to be that women with a mission could never marry. That's all changed, thank heaven. There's nothing to stop you, these days, from having a career *and* a family - *if* that's what you'd like. Running them alongside each other. Letting them both influence each other.

"I think we all have different lessons to learn while we're here. And how well we learn them dictates how well we do. I guess my lesson has been that you can't do it all! My life lesson is to surrender. Accept. That what we do is not more important than who we are. And it's who we become in the doing of what we do that's the most important thing. It's so easy to get caught up in the doing, and forget about the being."

Marigold sat back in her chair chewing her lip thoughtfully as Clare continued, "When I think of my most successful pieces, they were all touched by my own experience of life. It took Tabitha to point this out to me. I know you mentioned it too, but it took another person saying the same thing to actually get through to me! Those pieces were informed by my perception of the person through a personal lens. Echo's mother, for instance. She didn't feature in the article, but her devotion to her daughter enhanced my view of Echo. And that's something I was able to inject - that Echo was lovable, despite what she was alleged to have done. And the piece about Tabitha - that was another one that got a huge response. I've known Tabs for so long that I could really understand her journey and see her joy. That's what I showed in the article, while I was apparently talking about her achievements. Do you see what I mean?" she asked earnestly.

"I think you're saying that you have to have a rounded life. That living with your nose in a book is not going to enable you to convey your learning to others. In a way that they'll readily accept."

"Very much that, yes. You can be the greatest scholar on the planet, but if no-one loves you, you're not going to be worth as much."

"I know you love me, Mum. And I do admire what you're doing - your independence. Not sure why you're trying to put me off?"

"Because I can see the mistakes I've made! I can see where I was heading down the wrong path!" Clare jumped forward in her chair to make the point. "You've made me see that. Being here. Making me see what's the most important thing in my life. Making me look at what I have to do to be in integrity with myself!

"I just hope that this view you had of me didn't colour your decision. I've been wracked with guilt over that the past few days. That I'd misled you. That you were trying to follow an ideal that is, in fact, flawed." She looked across at her daughter with feeling.

"Oh, don't you feel guilty too!" Marigold said vehemently, seeing the anguish in her mother's face, "I've felt guilty enough all along. For falling for someone so thoughtlessly, for 'getting caught', for endangering my plans for my life. That's where I felt guilty. Putting it right has assuaged that guilt. I know there are lots of people who will think I've made it worse and I should now feel ultra-guilty. That's their perception and they're entitled to it. But I'll keep my own counsel. For me this chapter is closed."

"You're right. Guilt helps no-one! Along with shame and blame - totally fruitless. The best we can ever do is what we think is right at the time. Then we have to live with that decision. It can't be changed." Clare was talking to her daughter, but she was also talking to herself. She saw clearly now what was right for her. She saw where she had gone wrong. She was going to be so busy, forging ahead with both sides of her life - each side feeding the experience of the other, making a harmonious whole. And she felt that she was beginning to convey this discovery to Marigold. It wasn't too late, for either of them!

25

The following week Clare dropped Marigold off at Peggy's. She greeted her mother briefly after all the hugs Peggy was giving her granddaughter finally finished. "I'll be back in a few hours, Mum," she said, climbing back into her car, "See you later." In her mirror she could see Peggy and Marigold going into the house, arms around each other, as she drove away. Doubtless Peggy had been baking that lemony cake with fluffy icing that she knew Marigold loved. She was a very thoughtful person. She smiled and turned her thoughts forward again.

As Clare drove through the gates of Echo's home, she saw that the paparazzi had abandoned their vigil, broken camp and were no longer at the gate. She smiled to herself - it was down to her piece that the hounds had been called off. There were a number of cars in the drive in front of the big house when she arrived. Clare loved social occasions and was keen to meet Echo again, and see who she'd assembled for her.

This time Echo's mother was included in the party, rather than being a guardian and doorkeeper as she was when Clare had visited previously. Her caution had been natural enough, Clare reflected, after the slating her daughter had been getting in the press. Today she greeted Clare with a smile, leading her into the room and furnishing her with a glass of champagne.

A young man was just coming to the end of a story, at which all the other guests laughed uproariously. Echo saw Clare and came towards her smiling her welcome, both hands outstretched. Her striking presence was back with her again - that elusive something that performers had.

"Look everyone!" she said happily, "Here's Clare - the person who rescued my reputation and gave me back my life."

They all turned to look at Clare, smiling and nodding greetings.

"No, really, Echo!" protested Clare. "All I did was show the side of you that people don't get to see so much."

"Don't do yourself down!" laughed Echo. "You made the ravening wolves at the door go and find someone else to torment. Here - let me introduce you ..." And she set about leading Clare round all her guests, introducing them and giving a brief hint at what each one did, most of them in the entertainment business. After everyone had met her, the man who'd been telling the story came over and started telling Clare more about himself. She was glad of this, as pop music was not something she followed, and she had little idea who most of these people were. Clearly she'd need to do some homework!

She'd expected a roomful of performers to be more noisy, more brash and pushy. But as she got to speak to more of them individually, she reflected on her performing friend Tabitha - how quiet and introverted she was, yet driven to express herself very differently when actually on a stage. And, of course, Melanie was a performer too - and yet no-one could be more self-effacing.

"Clare, I want you to meet Bryan," Echo said after Clare had chatted with a number of the guests, taking her by the arm and leading her across the room. "You remember those books you were looking at last time you were here? Well, Bryan wrote the book that really got me on the right road - that one with the orange spine you can see over there on the shelf."

"Hello Bryan!" said Clare, and found herself quickly deep in conversation with this interesting writer, as Echo glided away back to the hubbub in the centre of the room.

"You were responsible for rescuing Echo from sinking, is that right?"

"It was easy enough to help the lovely Echo," he said. "She's a very willing learner. I guess she'd arrived at a time in her life when things needed careful adjustment."

"What she was doing wasn't working?" asked Clare with interest.

"She's young. It's very easy to get swept off your feet with all the adulation and praise and razzamatazz. She was in danger of drowning, yes. There are plenty of vultures around who are only too eager to see you fall from grace."

"I saw a bunch of them with their cameras outside the gate recently. Nasty to have to deal with."

"But I understand you were instrumental in getting that lot to move on. The piece you wrote putting the record straight ..."

"I was so impressed with Echo when I met her. There's obviously so much to her - much more than you might expect from a pop star who has been whisked up the charts. The piece wrote itself!" She smiled - knowing that a fellow writer would hear the nonsense in that statement, but understand what she meant. "But you've been working with her for a while, haven't you?"

"Yes. And it's been a pleasure. It helps me to keep my feet on the ground too. The thing is that the culture will sweep you away, take what it wants and spit out the pips. We all need to keep a balance ... "

"Ah, the elusive 'balance'," laughed Clare. "Isn't that what we hear we should all be seeking?"

"There's nothing wrong in devoting yourself to your art, your craft - your calling. But it has to be kept in check. Given a place - albeit an important place! - then kept there," Bryan smiled. "You can't have it swamping you entirely, taking over your life, colouring your judgments."

Clare shifted her glass from one hand to the other, then took a thoughtful sip, listening to Bryan as he went on.

"It's wrong to sacrifice yourself to someone or something else. And it's just as wrong to sacrifice part of your life to another part. You have to have a purpose in life: this is what brings happiness. Denying that purpose can never lead to a feeling of wholeness and satisfaction."

Echo had returned quietly and joined in here. "I was playing the part of the pop star to the extent that the rest of my life was denied. I was losing touch with who I was, and becoming what the masses demanded of me. It was resulting in loss of purpose, a loss of clarity really." She tossed her famous hair and added, "I'm all about seeking clarity! And you can see how much happier I am now that I'm putting these principles into action." She made a gesture that took in the broad sweep of the room and her friends. "I was way ahead of the public perception of me. It took them an age to catch up to how I had changed. And you were instrumental in this." She smiled warmly at them both. "So I thank you, Bryan, for helping me find my clarity! And you, Clare, for seeing it, then showing everybody."

"She's truly a remarkable young woman," Clare observed to Bryan as Echo left to talk to another guest.

"She's lived an awful lot of life in a very short time," he said, gazing after her. "And she was in danger of going down the accepted route for pop stars. Of believing her own press. And she's not only avoided that catastrophic plunge, but she's become a really strong person through it. She's a role-model for the upcoming wannabes."

"She has hidden depths - well, not so hidden, if you take the time to listen to her. Do you think she'll become one of the greats of pop music? That in forty years she'll be grey-headed pop royalty?"

"Could well be," he smiled. "Once you can sort out your inner demons, you become unstoppable. And then all you want to do is put out a helping hand to others, to draw them up with you."

"Hence your book?"

"Yep." He took a sip of his champagne and turned to her, "You must have a book inside you, with all the work you do?"

"I'm beginning to allow that thought, yes. If I'm good enough ..."

"Aha! There's something you need to address right away. People who aren't good enough seldom doubt themselves in that way. It's those who really *are* good enough who question their own abilities." He smiled enigmatically, as a big burst of laughter from across the room caused them to go and re-join the main group.

The lunch went well. Clare enjoyed meeting these people and trying to work out how they managed their gifts - or completely failed to manage them and ended up in trouble, like Echo had. She could see some who were just rescuing themselves from slipping down the wrong track. Echo had something like a commune going here, where she attracted followers who were genuine, not sycophants.

As she was escorted to the door by Echo's mother a couple of hours later, she thought about how 'normal' these extraordinary people were, deep down. They all had the same needs and wants as everyone else. They just had a beast to feed, in the form of their desire to perform, to show off their art, express the gifts which they hadn't asked for, but had to live with. And it was when ambition and talent got out of balance that people got the wrong idea about them. And some of these performers got the wrong idea about themselves too. That was so easy to understand. A young star, inexperienced in real life, and surrounded with fame and adulation, manipulators and leeches, was quite likely to believe their own publicity, becoming a caricature of themselves.

Clare came away with several names in her notebook, of people she'd like to contact later. Some of them had asked her to feature them, put the record straight about them. The story-teller she'd met early on turned out to be the leader of a band who was known for his outrageous stage behaviour - smashing up the stage, insulting the audience, very suggestive body movements. All done before, thought Clare, and it was accepted well enough when there was a true talent behind it all. He was known as Bazza, and was apparently very famous. And yet he was polite and courteous, and evidently well-educated and well-read. While his stage persona got him up the charts, he was keen to show the softer side of himself. He had a girl with him who was clearly special to him - not just another groupie. Clare got the impression he wanted to settle down, and was thinking of his future family. This would make a very interesting piece! She thought for a moment of Marigold, old beyond her years, refined in the fire of life and experience, and keen to live a 'real' life.

So, exhilarated from spending a couple of hours with such an abundance of talent, her head was buzzing with all the possibilities when she set off for Peggy's house, to catch up with her own mother and her daughter. Families seemed to be playing a big role in her day today, especially mothers and daughters. In fact mothers or fathers and their daughters had become quite a theme for her over the past few weeks.

26

She arrived to find the two women in her life as thick as thieves. The day was mild for the time of year, and they were sitting in the garden with a blanket over their knees, watching the antics of the hens pecking about and racing after insects, enjoying the fallen apples. The flock made a pleasant sight, some red, some white with black stripes down their necks, and one pretty lavender-coloured bird called Bluebelle who looked particularly plump and contented.

"How did it go, dear?" asked Peggy, turning to see Clare striding across the lawn towards them.

"It was really good - I got to meet several of the stars of the moment, including Bazza." The silence that greeted this statement showed that neither of them had a clue who Bazza was.

"You don't know Bazza?" she turned to Marigold, laughing. "Ah, you're not as up-to-date as your old mother! But really, Marigold ... what stone have you been living under? I think you need to get out more."

"I know a lot of the Irish bands - I really prefer traditional music," said Marigold. "What's this Bazza like? Here, let me make some fresh coffee - have some of Amma's gorgeous lemon cake. You can tell me about your famous pop-star friends in the car! You chat to Amma." She picked up the tray and headed indoors.

"Well?" asked Clare, once she was out of earshot.

"I'm so glad to see her back to her normal self," said Peggy. "It's an awful thing altogether. But it's finished now. She tells me you've had some long, deep, conversations together."

"This whole business has made me look at my own life in a new way," began Clare, gazing at the distant fields she could glimpse through the trees, harrowed now and looking for all the world like rich brown corduroy. "We all affect each other. We can't just plough our own furrow and not expect it to have a knock-on effect. I can see now what you've silently been trying to tell me these last two years." She watched two of the hens arguing cluckily over one blade of grass for a moment, then went on, "Dad was a very strong character."

"That he was," said Peggy flatly.

"What do you think Dad would have thought of all this?"

"Well, he wasn't really as black and white in his thought as you seem to think he was ..." said Peggy thoughtfully.

"But he was pretty black and white when it came to pulling us out of school!"

"Yeah. That was him all right. Thing is, he thought that the Master was a blackguard and a chancer. And he didn't want his children having anything to do with him."

"Whatever got him started on that? I can't remember."

"I don't really know, but I think it was probably that the Master didn't bend the knee enough to our local poet genius. But that makes Michael sound very small-minded, which he wasn't ... Well, I think you did well out of it in the end, he wasn't wrong about teaching you at home. All the things that you learnt: they stood you in good stead for the rest of your life, possibly better than having arguments with other kids and getting into trouble for not doing your homework."

"Yeah, you could be right. Still I'm glad that Marigold and Rollo were at decent schools all along. It's certainly done them well."

They fell to silence as a couple more of the hens had a noisy altercation - doubtless over ownership of some tiny insect. A big white hen strode off with the prize in her beak, dodging the others who clucked their protest loudly.

"Ma, tell me something," said Clare. "If things had worked out differently, did Dad think .. well what did Dad think would become of me?"

"Well, he knew you were bright enough to go to university - but he assumed that you'd do just the same as I did really, meet somebody better and pack it all in and devote yourself to child-rearing."

"That is just *so* old-fashioned! And yet he made himself out to be an artist."

"Yes, and despite the streams of brave Irish heroines all through history he did think that."

"Then that's pretty disappointing. I would say I have the highest hopes of Marigold making it - even in a man's world. I hope that if she wants to she'll have children too, but I want her to be true to her abilities - true to herself. As I wasn't.

"You see, I'd never realised how much some of the things Da told me had affected me. Burrowed deep into my psyche and lodged there. I was living my life according to the edicts dished out by him, Mícheál Ó Súilleabháin, the great poet. But he came from a different time, a different culture. What he thought was right may have been right for him. But it wasn't right for me. I've been looking to see what else I've always accepted blindly as gospel. And I've found a few things ..." She picked up the end of the blanket and draped it over her lap.

"What have you found?" prompted Peggy, after a pause.

"I always thought that I couldn't be a genuine artist at the same time as running a household, rearing a family. I didn't think that out loud, of course. Putting it into words would have blown its cover, shown it to be nonsense! But the belief was inside me, a program running in the background, dictating my decisions. I see that as madness now, of course. I only have to look around me to see people combining the two - even Bazza today. And I thought everything had to be perfect, or not do it at all. I had to be the best."

"You were always competitive, alright," said her mother.

"What I've seen recently, is that you can't deny your love. Love is there, and you have to allow it expression. And that love informs your art. Instead of thinking you can't be creative *and* truly love, I now see how you actually can't do the one without the other!"

Peggy watched her, listening. The hens were quiet now and Clare's eyes narrowed as they followed an owl swooping silently above the fence at the end of her garden.

"And I'm seeing it all over the place. Once I've become aware of these thoughts, I wonder how I could have been so blind for so long. Everywhere I look there are people managing to get the balance right in their lives. And people who are aware of what's eluded me, and who understand its importance." She turned away and bent over to pluck some grass.

"How's Rollo doing?" asked Peggy, after a pause, as Clare absently shredded the blades of grass she'd picked.

"Well," said Clare, "Rollo's a bit of a dark horse. Still waters run deep, that's Rollo. You'd think he's just a scientist who's all in his head. But there's a lot of feeling there, and he is very, very fond of his sister, which is so touching."

"You're right, and it's what you brought them up to be. That one lies firmly at your door, Clare."

"Thanks, Mum. I did something right."

"You've done lots of things right, my special. Lots of things. Don't beat yourself up over things that you may not have done. You have done so much. And those kids worship you."

Clare smiled shyly, and turned to see Marigold appearing in the doorway with the newly-laden tray. "And I really want Marigold to see this about balance too. I feel that I might have influenced her decision ..."

"Water under the bridge," said Peggy firmly. "Guilt and regret are pointless."

Marigold put the tray down on the low wooden table by the bench, and started pouring the coffee.

"Marigold," said Peggy, passing a mug to Clare, "tell your mother what you were saying about the art classes."

"Oh yes - here you go Amma - my drawing is kind of ok," she began as she passed Peggy a mug and moved another creaky wooden garden chair closer to the table, "but if it were better I could do the illustrations of the artefacts myself for my papers. So I thought I'd join the art club at uni and get better at it. I'd meet some more people there too - different people, not just from my Faculty." She smiled at her mother, acknowledging that she realised a bit of diversification would be a good thing.

"Your drawing is more than ok!" said Peggy. "What about all those pictures of horses you used to send me? Not to mention your cat - what was her name? Gertie? Trudie! That's it." She smiled at the memory.

"Ah, Trudie - she was a great cat!" sighed Marigold.

"I think that's a really good idea, Marigold," said Clare. "And you know what," she slowly put her mug down on the little table, "that gives me an idea! I always used to love singing, but I haven't really done any since school. I wonder if there's some choir I could join? One that would accept a rubbish singer!"

"Why did you ever stop singing if you love it so? I do remember you used to sing as you made the dinner - weird stuff in Latin," said Marigold.

"Yes, I did love that kind of music. I guess I thought I wasn't good enough ..." Clare gazed at the fields beyond the trees. "I always want to do everything perfectly. And at that time I was focussed on being a wife and mother and hostess." She took a sip of her coffee and brought herself back to the present. "And I'm learning that perfection is really not a good thing to aim for. Life is there to be enjoyed - every bit of it, the good and the not-so-good." She smiled meaningfully at her daughter, then laughed.

"Look at us both, planning new things we'll have to learn almost from scratch!"

"Oh, this is fun! So what about you, Amma? Will you join in? What are you going to do to branch out?"

"Well," Peggy said slowly, "we're pretty rural here. I've lived here for years but I don't really know anything about the history of the place. There are some fascinating old churches and ancient barns I've seen on my walks. I bet there's some sort of local history society ...." She turned to her granddaughter and declared firmly, "I'll look into it."

"I'll keep you to that," laughed Marigold happily. "Look at us - all bursting forth to new parts of our lives."

27

Before leaving the country, there was just time for one more social call for Marigold.

"I know how much your friends mean to you, Mum," she'd said as they drove home from Peggy's, "and I'd love to meet them. Is there time for that before I go? I want to know I'm leaving you in good hands," she smiled as she turned to her. Clare felt the tables turning, that Marigold wanted to look after her, as she wanted to care for Marigold. It was a warm and lovely realisation, that all that love and care she had lavished on her children could actually be reciprocated by the adults they were becoming.

So Clare had managed to hastily arrange a dog walk with Tabitha and Melanie and their dogs, which they could just fit in on their way to the airport the next day. She still hadn't mentioned to them the true purpose of Marigold's visit. That could keep till another time. She may have to tread carefully round this delicate subject for Tabitha, whose childlessness had been such a blight on her life. For now it sufficed to tell them that her daughter was much better after her break, and was eager to return to college again.

They met at a car park on the edge of some glorious woodland, carefully chosen as being both *en route* to the airport and sparing Melanie having to drive right into town. The scene was mesmerising in its Autumn colours. It turned out that Tabitha was near enough the same shoe-size as Marigold, so she was able to bring a spare pair of wellies for her. Marigold protested she'd be fine in her own shoes which were fairly robust, but Tabitha persuaded her that spending the next five hours in wet shoes till she arrived back at her hall was really not a good idea. It was a still day, and sunny though cold, and the coloured carpet of leaves crunching under their feet was a delight.

Marigold loved meeting the dogs - Cariad was delighted to find a new victim for her love - and surprisingly she made firm friends with Heidi, usually so shy of people.

"You've got the touch," said Melanie admiringly.

"That's from a childhood spent nurturing cats and ponies!" laughed Clare. "Marigold was always the sensitive one."

"What better way to grow up?" mused Tabitha. "I'm sure Simon made a huge impact on me - how I deal with other people, how I see life ..."

"Simon?" asked Marigold.

"Big old-fashioned lollopy spaniel," said Tabitha, smiling fondly at the memory of her childhood friend. "We were inseparable. He was the same age as me, so I'd never known life without him. That made it even more devastating when he died."

"They just don't live long enough," sighed Melanie.

"There was a writing competition at school," Tabitha went on. "You had to write about Roads. I chose to write about Simon, who was all I could think about at that time, and I called it The Road of Life. Yeah," she laughed, "corny, I know, but I was only twelve ... It was still a very raw loss for me, so I wrote with great feeling. I actually reached the top three and had to read my essay out in front of the whole school!"

"You never told me you wrote!" exclaimed Clare.

"Hardly writing," demurred Tabitha. "Rather a mawkish story about a dog. Not anything like what you do."

"Still, you should write again - perhaps a play for Shooting Stars?"

"Maybe," she conceded, with a distant look as this new idea was clearly taking root in her mind. "Though that essay was born out of the loss of the most important thing in my life at the time .."

"Did you not have brothers and sisters?" asked Marigold.

"Yes - there's William. But he was several years older than me, and a small gap is quite large when you're young. He was usually off doing different things." She kicked a pine cone for the dogs to chase after. "But I was always happy on my own," she smiled, and added, "as long as I had plenty to read."

As they walked in the cool air, Marigold asked the two friends about their lives. Tabitha's work with children's drama she found fascinating, and could understand, but she said to Melanie, "I had no idea you could spend your days dancing with dogs and teaching other people how to!"

"Well, the dancing bit is for my pleasure, really. I run ordinary dog training classes. Though I don't really like that term - training. You don't have 'family training' or 'children training'! What I aim to do is show people how to relate to their dogs in a way which brings both of them pleasure. There are so many outdated ideas still, about how you have to control your dog, punish him, keep him in his place, and so on. You'd never do that with your family. Some of the methods people still teach are positively brutal! But it doesn't have to be like that. Here - have you heard Tabs or me shout at our dogs today? Have you seen anything but happiness from all of us?"

"Nope. Definitely not. But your dogs are so good. Don't some dogs jump up on people, steal food, chew things?"

"Only if they haven't been shown another way," said Melanie, matter-of-factly. "Our dogs would be just as bad if we just let them get on with it. They *are* only dogs, after all!"

"So you don't think they're kind of furry people?" asked Marigold. "Some people seem to treat their dogs like children."

"No. They're dogs! Another species - and we're honoured to be able to share our lives with them, and live this symbiotic existence together."

They walked on in silence as they all absorbed this, still scuffing the leaves covering the path.

"I was really nervous when I first got in touch with Melanie to help teach Esme her sausage-stealing role for our play," chipped in Tabitha. "I'd had experience of ghastly so-called dog training in the past. And I was absolutely decided to show her the door if she did anything I didn't like to my dogs. Do you remember, Melanie?"

"I remember the suspicion I was greeted with, yes!" Melanie laughed. "And how quickly you warmed to what I was showing you when you saw how happy the dogs were. That was when you had Luigi too." There was a moment's silence as the three older women remembered Luigi and his unfortunate end. Marigold looked questioningly at Clare, clearly feeling the sudden tension in the air. Clare gave a little shake of her head. She would tell Marigold more about Tabitha's past and her sweet old dog Luigi later.

Tabitha took a deep breath and went on, "Once you know how to reach the dog's mind, and use science instead of old wives' tales, it's easy to change them so they fit in with our world and can enjoy it with us. Same goes for children. I've learnt a lot from Melanie and her studies of the science of dog behaviour that helps me every day with the children I work with."

"Actually, she knew a lot of it already," interrupted Melanie. "She just didn't know that they'd proved it all in university studies. She's a natch!"

Tabitha smiled, as Marigold fell in beside her and asked.

"So what exactly do you do, Tabitha. I know you're at the National Drama School ..."

"I run the Junior Academy there. And I still have my little school out in the sticks where it all started - Shooting Stars. What exactly do I do?" She took the stick Rhys was offering, snapped off the soft twiggy part of it and tossed it for him, amidst a flurry of tails from all four dogs. "Officially I teach them drama, acting, performing. What I'm actually doing is building their confidence, giving them dignity, giving them a place in the world where they don't doubt themselves." The stick came back, this time carried by Esme who was turning her head to keep it away from Cariad. As she threw it again, into a heap of leaves, Tabitha went on, "Stealth personal development! Bit like Melanie really. People come to her because, as you say, their dog is stealing stuff, or jumping on them, or annoying them in some other way."

"And I get them to change what they're doing *to* their dog - get them to enjoy doing things *with* their dog instead. Once we shift the balance, the annoyances become very easy to fix," Melanie said.

"Dog personal development!" laughed Marigold.

"It's my passion to help as many dogs as possible to enjoy better lives. And I can only reach the dogs through their owners. So yes - it's dog-owner personal development, really."

"You both have very clear missions in what you do," said Clare, joining in again. "I think that's where I've been lacking. I knew I wanted to write, wanted to change the world, but I was looking at it very narrowly. I'm seeing now that my gifts lie in being able to show the inner thoughts of a person, show what really makes them tick. And it's through my own relationships with people that I'm able to do this. Can't exist in a vacuum," she added, quietly, thinking again of what she wanted to impart to Marigold, that it was possible to pursue your passion without sacrificing the whole of your life to it.

"You've been single-minded in developing your career these last twelve months or so," Tabitha said. "You've done so well. You should congratulate yourself. But yes - good time to reflect on where you really want to go with it. Sometimes we need something to jolt us off our rails in order to see which rails we actually want to be on."

"Ooh, Tabitha! Profound," said Melanie, watching Clare at the same time.

"Clare knows all about this. Without her help last year ... I'm not sure where I'd be." She smiled warmly at Clare. They all stopped walking for a moment, and Marigold said quietly, "Was I the jolt for you, Mum?"

Clare looked up at her three companions, surprised to find tears welling in her eyes. She thought of what Echo had said to her the day before, 'You've helped me in seeking the purpose in my life, seeking clarity. And I think I've found it.'

"Yes, my lovely girl," she said, throwing an arm round her daughter's shoulders. "You've been the making of me."

28

A few weeks after Marigold's departure everything was back to normal for Clare, except for one thing: she didn't feel the need to try so hard. Her first choir practices, airing her rusty singing voice and remembering how to read music again, had been liberating. She was thoroughly enjoying being a junior choir member, ready to learn from the eager choirmaster and the better singers.

In fact, she felt relaxed as she went into Joanne's office for their editorial meeting. Thanks to her second visit to Echo, she had pages of ideas to submit, and was bubbling with enthusiasm. While she was still full of eagerness, she found she'd been able to pace herself better.

"You see," she explained to Joanne, "I was getting several deadlines jammed together, then nothing for weeks! I know it's inevitable to a degree, when you're fitting in with other people, but I'm scheduling much better now. I've even allocated 'me-time' - that's a first!"

"I don't want you getting cosy and comfortable," Joanne stared at her with a steely gaze over the top of her red glasses.

"I haven't lost my edge, if that's what you mean! I'm still hungry, just making more sense of it. Not trying so hard to impress anyone."

"You don't need to: I have news about the Social Impact Award - you've been shortlisted!"

"Wow!" Clare beamed at Joanne. "That will be quite a feather in my cap already - never mind the possibility of winning it!"

"What's more, your dog piece has been syndicated. It's even gone to the other side of the world - let me see ..." she put her glasses on and moused about on her screen, "South Africa, Tasmania, Japan ... You're reaching new audiences. So I want more like that, if you don't mind," she smiled at Clare, showing her softer side in her pleasure.

They went through Clare's list, and Joanne was quick to pick out Bryan's name. "This looks interesting - as long as you can relate it to what you're doing in your other pieces. You're developing a brand for sensitive investigative journalism, the velvet claw in the iron glove," she gave a wry smile at her own joke, "You want to stay on-brand as far as you can."

They bent their heads over the list again, and Joanne triumphantly put her finger on the series Clare was suggesting, of mothers and daughters and how they affected each other.

"This I like," she said. "Get started on this straight away. Hmm, let me think ..."

Clare waited for her to come out with something more, but Joanne simply handed the paper back to her and said, "You've got plenty there."

So they settled the schedule for the next month, making sure Harriet would be able to work with her for the photos - "She's so good at getting just what I'm after," explained Clare, "She gets me." Joanne leant back in her chrome swivel chair, put down her red glasses, and said, "I seem to remember you talking about a longer piece, a novel. How's that going?"

"I've actually started on it, at last." Clare showed her pleasure and hid her surprise as best she could. "This is one of the issues I've resolved, along with scheduling some me-time. I was waiting for the perfect moment. Never going to happen. So I decided to just jump in and get going with it!"

"So what's your theme?" asked Joanne.

"It's about ... it's about a woman trying to succeed in a man's world - and failing - till she discovers it's not about competing with them, trying to be the best, but doing what she can do that no-one else can. It's about self-belief, really."

"Now, I wonder where that idea came from?" smiled Joanne. "I'd be interested to have a look when you've got anything ready to show."

So Clare was walking on air once more when she left her Editor's office. And her sunny mood enfolded Nat as she reached his desk. She perched on the end of it as she so often did, while he regaled her with stories about what he was planning for Christmas for his little family - not so little any more, as he proudly announced that his wife was expecting another child in the Spring.

"That's so thrilling, Nat! I bet you're all excited about the baby."

Nat smiled like the cat who'd got the cream. "Molly's the most excited, as a matter of fact. She's only seven, but sees herself as the perfect second-in-command when it comes to baby-minding. She'll be very good at it, I think. Alison's finding this pregnancy easier already, with Molly so eager to help. It's very cute, hearing a seven-year-old saying, 'You need to put your feet up, Mummy,' though she still has plenty of time to be seven and totally self-centred, I'm glad to say. Tom has little interest though," he added.

"How old's Tom again?"

"Four."

"He has much more important things to think about!" laughed Clare. "It'll all work out fine."

"He did say, 'It had better be a boy or you can send it back'." Nat laughed happily.

"Once the older girls had got over the shock and embarrassment that their parents had 'done that', even at our great age! - they got really excited. It's helping deal with teenage issues, as they don't want to upset their Mum by fighting and being difficult. They're really growing up ... it seems to have been a great idea all round!"

As she walked away from his desk, Clare thought of Tabitha's friend Gerard, another man who was devoted to his family. And Melanie's story about her father popped into her mind. Clare usually wrote about women and their struggles and victories, but here was another subject she could happily dive into - looking at the family from the man's view-point. She was pondering this when she bumped into Nick. He gave her a big smile, saying "Hey stranger! You look terrific."

She hadn't spoken to him since she'd had to cancel their trip. "Hey Nick!" She gave him a quick hug and a beaming smile. "I'm sorry about the hotel thing. Did you get fixed up alright after all?"

"Nope. Couldn't find anyone as tempting as you," he smiled. "Here, got a minute for a coffee?"

Clare nodded and they headed to the canteen - or staff restaurant as Zenith liked to call it. She was glad to spend a little time with Nick. She did like him, and felt bad about letting him down. Though, to be honest, she'd forgotten all about that weekend with everything else that had happened.

The canteen was on the top floor of the tall Zenith building, and had a view through its huge windows of the city below them, giving the denizens the impression that they looked over the world, and ruled it. They chatted about Nick's events work, and Clare told him about the Award she was up for.

"Congratulations!" he said, with genuine warmth. "Always thought you were a high flyer ... How about dinner, next week?"

Clare looked steadily at him. She had allowed this relationship to develop the way it had. She couldn't blame Nick for happily taking what was offered. She liked him, and felt sure there was more to him than she had seen so far. "I'd like that, Nick. But ... can we back-pedal a bit, go a bit slower? I've been doing a lot of thinking lately, I need to keep myself ... to myself a bit more."

He got the message, loud and clear. "You know I enjoy your company, Clare. Your accent melts my heart." He affected a really bad Irish accent and adopted a serious face, but the twinkle in his eye gave him away. "Sure. Dinner. Dinner only. I get it. Don't want to interfere with the progress of the go-getter!"

"It's not that so much ... I had shaken off the shackles - not that there was anything bad about my marriage - but I went full steam ahead into this new life, keeping relationships in what I thought were their proper place. But now ... I'm more balanced. More sensible. Not rushing headlong."

They fixed a date, and Clare left the building feeling much more sure of what she was doing. Everything seemed to be falling into place, she thought, as she made her way home. Rollo had arranged a three-way call for this afternoon, with Marigold on the line too, so she had to be back promptly.

She made good time, and was able to get some phone calls in before their meeting. In the run-up to Christmas, there were lots of interviews for her to arrange. Nobody would give her any time after about the middle of December, so she had to cram a month into half a month. But she wouldn't be idle after that. The interview with Bryan was turning into a big piece, and she'd allocated time from Christmas Eve onwards to work on her novel. Jonathan was having both children over Christmas. They'd come to a kind of easy peace with Aisling, so their few days there would not be fraught, she hoped.

She thought of Peggy, and how she'd been quietly beavering away behind the scenes to unite her family. It had been quite a *tour de force,* and she realised now how much help her mother had given her in resolving the issues with her own daughter. It was this mother-daughter thing again - it just kept showing up wherever she looked. She grabbed her laptop and made some notes. This was going to be a long series! It had the makings of something really good. She could take people from all walks of life - she could even interview Echo's mother! She had so many ideas coming to her now. It was as if a floodgate had been opened, she just had to catch and filter the ideas, join them together, stay 'on-brand' as Joanne put it.

And a little later it was with satisfaction that she closed the notes she'd made and with a big beam of pleasure looked at the screen with both her children there in front of her.

"Has Amma talked to you about after Christmas, Mum?" asked Rollo.

"Yes, she has. You're both going to stay with her for a bit before term starts again, right?"

"Some of our cousins will be there too for a big do she's arranging. It'll be good to see them again. Haven't seen any of them since that party you gave in Brownestown years ago. Young Michael has five kids now, so it'll be a houseful!"

Clare smiled at the name 'Young Michael'. Old habits die hard.

"Yeah, I'm really looking forward to going," said Marigold. "Amma says there's an important ancient site not too far from her - a chalk horse carved in the side of a hill. It dates from the Bronze Age and I can't wait to visit it!"

"Perhaps I can come too?" asked Clare. "I'll be joining you for a couple of days too."

"Ohh!" they both chorused. "That'll be great," said Rollo. "Gives me more time to get your present!" The children laughed and Clare smiled happily.

They were both young and beautiful and full of promise. And they were so natural with each other, and with her. It had taken Marigold's major life crisis to make her see what she had been missing by staying apart from them. She'd always hated the thought of being the pushy mother, always nagging her children, ringing them up and demanding their attention. But she had to admit she hadn't been all that open to them either. They had ended up not wanting to impinge on her, invade her space. She had been distant.

But now they were taking matters into their own hands. These calls were becoming a frequent fixture, though they couldn't always manage the same time, and usually it was a two-way call. They were likely to text or ring at random times too. Rollo in particular enjoyed sending photos he'd taken of unusual sights and details: his scientific mind was very observant. And Marigold had sent images of some of her new drawings. The thought that they wanted to share these everyday things with her filled her with love. Instead of resenting their intrusion while she pursued what she had always considered more important things, she looked forward to their calls. She felt their warmth around her, and it brought more warmth to her writing too, less tension. Clare saw that her job with them was not done. Just as she turned to Peggy for help when she needed it, Rollo and Marigold could turn to her. She was still an important part of their lives. She had a place, and she was determined to live up to it now.

29

As the weather grew colder, Clare's life seemed to get warmer. Joanne had come up trumps, despite all the messing around Clare had caused her.

"I saw something in you when you first submitted your work," she said on the phone that day. "And you've proved me right - again," she laughed lightly. "You've repaid my faith in you. You're in the final three for the Award!"

Clare was overcome for a moment. It was hard to believe! She'd only been in the business for eighteen months or so, and already she was making waves.

"So you'll have to get yourself some glad rags for the event. And an escort. Got anyone in mind?"

Clare thought this was the perfect occasion to invite Nick, who had behaved impeccably on their recent dates. She was seeing him now as a friend rather than a boyfriend, and they both seemed to enjoy their meet-ups. He would certainly be an asset, events being his thing. Why not show him off?

And she still hadn't worn that dress she'd bought for their aborted time away together. It had been quite forgotten in the turmoil following

Marigold's dramatic arrival at her door and was still wrapped in its tissue paper. It would be perfect for this ceremony!

"Oh, and get your chum Harriet to do some photos of you. You're going to need them for your new column." Joanne waited in the silence while Clare absorbed this news.

"My own column!" she gasped, "Joanne! Thank you! When do I start?"

"In the February edition. That latest series of articles you suggested - the mother-daughter thing - I think that would make a great launch. Accounts will be in touch with you with your new rates. How's the novel?"

After their friendly chat, Clare was still on a cloud when the doorbell rang. Tabitha and Melanie were due to come round this evening, after rehearsals at the Junior Academy. Melanie was doing a short piece with Rhys in the winter performance.

"Can I bring Rhys up to your flat please?" Melanie had asked anxiously on the phone when they'd arranged it. "Heidi will be at home with Dad. I don't like to leave a dog in the van in the city. They can steal the van if they must, but I couldn't relax knowing Rhys was out there."

So it was lateish by the time they arrived, busy, pink-cheeked, and energised by the rehearsal. The usually-quiet room was suddenly full of life and movement, especially as Rhys was keen to explore every nook and cranny. Clare had prepared a meal for them, and had made a peach drink instead of wine - she knew Melanie would have a late drive home. And she'd put some chopped cheese and ham in a bowl for Melanie to give to Rhys, as an honoured guest.

"It's going really well!" enthused Tabitha, as they helped themselves to the food. "Tonight was the first time the children had seen Melanie's routine."

"I bet they loved it!" said Clare, passing a plate to Melanie.

"They were so excited!" she said as she took the proffered food. "It was quite a test for Rhys. Competitions are tense, but the spectators are usually adult, and a bit blasé about the whole thing. So this level of fizz and activity was new for him - you know how children can't keep still. I don't know how you manage them, Tabs," she added, ripping off a chunk of bread.

"Just the same way you do with your dogs," replied Tabitha as she buttered her bread. "I channel all their energy into what I want. This is where they grow so much in confidence. They find they can control how they feel and what they do, and make it work for them. D'you know," she added, "this year's intake into the Drama School included *all* my Juniors who wanted to continue? Every single one who applied got through on the first interview! I was so proud of them."

"I bet the Drama people were pleased, getting new students who are half-cooked already?" Clare topped up their glasses.

"Well, that was their plan in the first place, actually. It was part of the Director's vision for the Academy, that it would be a feeder for the main college. And it's worked out really well. You see, the parents can see early on just how hard their kids have to work to get anywhere in this business. It's a kind of filtering system for applications."

"Haven't you got something happening with your other school? I don't know how you fit it all in ..."

"Yes - the Christmas performance: a high point in the calendar for Shooting Stars! Melanie's doing her thing there too."

"We're so much in demand!" laughed Melanie, waving her fork in as nonchalant a manner as she could manage.

"The children were enraptured when they first saw Rhys working," Tabitha went on, "and their parents have been hearing about it for weeks so they're curious to see what it's all about. Tickets sold out so quickly that we had to put on a second performance! Sally - who as you know does all the real work there - is thrilled to bits with how her figures are balancing. She's actually earning a decent income from the School. Things are so different from a year ago," she added, gazing at the large bowl of salad in front of her. "So between the Academy and Shooting Stars we get double the performances, for half the work."

"And that one's local for me," said Melanie after swallowing a mouthful of smoked salmon, "so it's a bit easier. Much smaller stage though in the village hall, so I've had to modify the routine to fit. It's all good learning!" Rhys had settled down beside her on a cushion Clare had tossed down for him, and Melanie turned to pass him a couple of lumps of cheese. The thump of his tail showed his appreciation.

"Harriet was asking about you the other day, Melanie," said Clare, taking a sip of her drink. "She really enjoyed zooming in on the action shots. How about inviting her to take photos at the performance, Tabitha? I'm sure the NDS could afford her."

"That's a *great* idea, Clare! Give me her details - I'll give her a ring. She seems very approachable - I met her at your photoshoot too, remember?"

They fell to comparing notes over their holiday plans, the busy build-up and the relaxing time after. It didn't surprise any of them to find that they had each planned work on a new project during the break.

Tabitha had an idea about private coaching for some of her students' parents that she wanted to investigate. "It's about the reality of showbiz and how best to support their children - partly inspired by your piece, Clare, the one about Echo and her mother."

"I'm working on a new series of workshops to offer my existing clients, to keep them in the loop," said Melanie. "It's part of the deal in my club - they pay a subscription for extra stuff."

"That sounds very canny," said Clare appreciatively. "You're quite the businesswoman!"

"I have to be now, after that big influx of clients on foot of your article about me. It's amazing - it makes life so much easier when I don't have to be scrabbling for money the whole time."

"I'm really happy for you - it's richly deserved: you're a find. And I'll be working on my novel," she added with a smile.

"I expect a starring role," laughed Melanie.

"It's the perfect time for making something new," said Tabitha, brushing some crumbs off her lap towards Rhys. "The phone doesn't ring! Or at least, if it does, I don't feel obliged to answer it."

"Will you be ok over Christmas, Clare?" asked Melanie. "We've got our dogs, and I've got Dad too. You won't feel lonely?"

"I'll do fine, don't worry. But you've given me an idea I've been turning over in my mind for a while now. I think I need to build up my nurturing side. Having someone to look after takes the focus off me-me-me. It's good for me to have someone else to think about. Ground myself. Make me more of a home-bird. So ... I'm going to get a kitten!"

Her friends crowed with delight over this, and both quickly offered to help mind the cat when Clare had to travel away for a night.

"The dogs won't eat it?" asked Clare nervously, though she was relieved to get the offer as she'd been wondering whether any of her neighbours - whom she hardly knew - would be able to help.

"Course not!" they both laughed. "Anyway," said Tabitha, "if you were away for the night I could just drop in after work and minister to the beastie, and visit again in the morning. Probably easier for the cat to stay at home. They're not as adaptable as dogs in that way: they're better off in a place they know. Where are you going to get one? It's not that easy, these days. Shelters can be so fussy."

"No problem," put in Melanie brightly. The farmer down the road from me always has kittens - you remember Tom, Tabitha?"

"Ah yes, it's like wading through a sea of black and white furry treacle, walking through his yard. He loves them - they're all over the place. They're working cats, of course, but I've found him on occasion sitting with one on his lap when he thought no-one was around."

"I'll ask him tomorrow whether he's got any kittens right now," said Melanie. "Maybe you'll have it in time for the break? Male or female?"

"I'd like a female, I think. Marigold always loved her cat Trudie - she'll enjoy the company when she visits here."

"And here's the big question - what are you going to call her?" asked Tabitha.

"Well I can't call her Tabby!" They all laughed at the idea. "So, yes, it is an important question, and I've given it a lot of thought. She's going to inspire me every time I look at her."

Tabitha and Melanie looked at her expectantly, while Rhys cocked an ear at the silence.

"I've decided to call her Clarity. Because that's what I've been seeking, and that's what I've found, at last."

~

Did you enjoy Clare's story? You can catch up with what happened next for her and her growing circle of friends and family here: https://beverley-courtney.ck.page/clarity-chapter

And to find out more about Tabitha, read the first book in this series of Dilemmas and Discovery, **Keeping Tabs – A women's fiction novel of Doubt, Dogs, and Determination** right now!

books2read.com/tabs

A note from the Author

I've enjoyed a wonderfully varied life, and - simply by following my passion - I've helped thousands of people to improve their lives through my teaching, my articles, and my nine ever-popular how-to dog training books, as a writer, coach, artist, and force-free dog trainer.

I have chosen to spend most of my life living in the countryside with my family and various animals - goats, sheep, chickens, donkeys, dogs, cats, an amazing parrot, and children (!) being chief among them.

Not afraid of handling difficult subjects, my accessible writing style with a dash of humour has already carried my often idiosyncratic ideas to many dog-owners looking for a kind way to be with their dogs (www.brilliantfamilydog.com/books). And this continued into my first novel, **Keeping Tabs**, where we lived through Tabitha's struggles to discover her true path in life. Now she has been joined by her friend Clare with a completely different set of struggles!

A common response from readers and students is, "It's so obvious when you put it like that!" In the same straightforward way I'm thrilled to be getting results for my clients in my coaching practice. If you are affected by any of the issues in this book, do visit www.beverleycourtney.com for ideas to help you move forward.

If you got this far in the book, you must have some thoughts about it! It would be great if you could hop over to the book store where you found it, and leave a brief review. And I'd love to hear from you by email too, at beverley@beverleycourtney.com where I read every one.

Beverley Courtney

BA (Hons) CPC ELI-MP CB&T2 APDT(UK) CBATI ABTC

Norfolk, England

Acknowledgments

I wouldn't have got very far without some serious wisdom and cheerleading from the indefatigable Erin Lindsay McCabe, so – many thanks, Erin!

And thanks also to my children, for always keeping me driving onwards (whether they know it or not).

Where can you find me?

www.beverleycourtney.com
www.brilliantfamilydog.com
www.beverleycourtney.com/author

facebook.com/beverleycourtneycoaching
instagram.com/beverley.courtney